C. D. ROSE

who's
who
when
every
one
is
someone
else

a novel

MELVILLE HOUSE UK
BROOKLYN • LONDON

Who's Who When Everyone Is Someone Else

Copyright © C. D. Rose, 2017
The right of C. D. Rose to be identified as the author of this work has been asserted
by him in accordance with the Copyright, Designs & Patents Act 1988.
First Melville House Printing: April 2018

Melville House Publishing
46 John Street
Brooklyn, NY 11201
and
8 Blackstock Mews
Islington
London N4 2BT

mhpbooks.com
facebook.com/mhpbooks
@melvillehouse

ISBN: 978-1-161219-713-5
ISBN: 978-1-61219-714-2 (eBook)

Library of Congress Cataloging-in-Publication Data
Names: Rose, C. D., author.
Title: Who's who when everyone is someone else / C. D. Rose.
Description: Brooklyn : Melville House, 2018. |
Identifiers: LCCN 2017055010 (print) | LCCN 2017057364 (ebook) | ISBN
   9781612197142 (reflow able) | ISBN 9781612197135 (softcover)
Subjects: | BISAC: FICTION / Humorous. | GSAFD: Humorous fiction.
Classification: LCC PS3618.O78284 (ebook) | LCC PS3618.O78284 W48 2018
   (print) | DDC 813/.6--dc23
LC record available at https://lccn.loc.gov/2017055010

Designed by Fritz Metsch

Printed in the United States of America
1 3 5 7 9 10 8 6 4 2

A CIP catalogue record for this book is available from the British Library

To all those who made this book possible.

You may not know who you are.

The storyteller: he is the man who could let the wick of his life be consumed by the gentle flame of his story.

—WALTER BENJAMIN

OR

Ten Lectures on Great Lost Books

*I*T WAS A *burning morning in late summer when I took my leave
of Clara, the sky distant and receding as if in sympathy, the few
wisps of cloud that had graced the dawn and reminded me of her
hair now scorched away by the sun, already so hot at this hour, at
this time of the year. I stood outside the Café Terminus and watched
her pass, knowing I would never see her again, knowing our worlds
had finally, definitively, utterly separated, and all that would be left
of us were improbable names scratched in hotel registers, a bundle
of letters bound by a ribbon hidden in the drawer to the left of her
bed, and a few bitter tears, long evaporated, leaving only their salty
trace on a handkerchief that may, for all I knew, have gone with her.
Memories, I should say, memories would last, but I knew she no
longer had any, and the few I possessed were treacherous, deceitful,
liars to themselves as well as to me.*

*I sipped the last of my coffee, now little more than a sad black
meniscus lining the bottom of the cup as her handsome wooden box
passed by, pulled, as her father had insisted, by four fine black horses
along the corso then out of town onto the cart track as far as the
cemetery which lay a good few kilometres from any living habitation,
its own walled and silent kingdom. As she slowly faded from view, I
knew I was now, finally, free. Free to take the opposite direction, to
turn away from her, from this town, from their whole world.*

It was time to take the train.

The station was a tawdry, flyblown little place, scarcely worthy of the name, one platform and a bucket in a shed claiming to be a restroom. Yet it mattered little, as the locomotive appeared on time, entering the town just as Clara would have been leaving it to the other side. While I have to admit that there was a certain grace and pomp in the manner of her departure, train travel, too, has its own romance. The hiss of steam, the burn of coal and grit, the immense breath of the engine as it heaves itself into motion, slowly building to the mighty speed that even such an old chugger as this one could muster. As we passed into open country I listened to the sound of the iron wheels on the steel rails, felt the slow rock of the carriages, watched the land speed by as if I were watching a film. The history of all this, I thought, the knowledge that the rails I travelled on had been forged by honest steelworkers and laid by burly immigrants, that the rock gorge I was now passing through had been hewn by brave engineers laying dynamite with their bare hands. How many had died in the construction of this marvel? The land fell away beneath me, the sound suddenly expanding as we passed over a bridge fashioned from a Roman aqueduct.

But finest of all was the anonymity. Here, I could be anyone I liked. Stepping aboard a train is stepping into a new world. The random strangers. The potential for chance encounter. Once the door is locked and the whistle blown, the departure is total. No one knew me; I knew no one. I could begin again.

~

I LET THE book drop onto my lap and felt its pages slap shut. I closed my eyes and wished for sleep, but none came. I'd hoped Enrico Cavaletti's *Train to the End of the Night* would be the perfect thing to accompany me on a long rail journey and at first the rhythms of the prose dutifully matched the rocking of the train I was on, but soon the long sentences merely bored me and I had to go over them time and again, unable to focus, not for the first time disappointed by the gaping juncture between a book and reality.

I'd turned to Cavaletti on the advice of a friend whose name I was now trying to recall so that I could ignore any future advice from him. "It's a fine example of train literature, " I remember an indistinct voice telling me, and scribbled Cavaletti's name in my notebook for future reference only to forget it again until I was embarking on a long rail journey myself. I'd thought of including it on the reading list I was drawing up, too, but on the evidence of its opening passage it seemed little more than a piece of early-twentieth-century schlock, its fancy prose giving away far too much right from the first page. It could go on the reserve list, I supposed.

Sadly, I had nothing else to hand, my only other books stuffed into one of the suitcases now stashed on a dangerously narrow overhead luggage rack. To get it down and open it up would have meant disturbing my fellow passengers, none of whom seemed the types to be disturbed without annoyance. I stared out of the window instead, and thought about how it wasn't the gap between the book and reality that had disappointed me, but rather my failure to allow what I had been reading to change the world I was in.

The world I was in at that point was a packed train now three hours late due to an unexplained and interminable stop in the middle of flat empty fields somewhere just over the border between two countries, neither of which I knew the first thing about. I was squashed into a back-aching seat next to a man who had the air of a distracted philosophy professor, and seemed to be sleeping off a heavy lunch. Across from me, another man was attempting to engage the other members of our compartment in conversation, but the two young women were content to whisper to each other and ignore him, while the final occupant, a nun of some order unknown to me, only nodded whenever he spoke to her and said not a word. Fortunately, as long as I read or pretended to read, I maintained the force field of the book-absorbed foreigner, one which no one attempted to break.

After what felt like several hours—but I concede may have been fewer—the train began again, slowly enough to let a few grey storage hangars emerge from the fog but rising to a steady trundle through a cluster of unimpressive tower blocks, which in turn gave way to spreading leafy suburbs before sinking into a tunnel of near-Stygian gloom, its brick and cement walls seeming remarkably free of graffiti. The tunnel then opened out into a glass-domed space, all light and iron tracery, pigeons swooping around the crosswork beams. A platform hove up alongside us as the train slowed, the film finishing. An ornate fin-de-siècle sign announced the name of our city, and the word "Terminus." The end.

~

AND SO I had arrived, a man in a battered hat with a bulky suitcase in each hand, suffering under an overcoat too heavy for the weather. I could have been that eternal migrant, the one slowly fleeing from some domestic turmoil, the man who'd shifted from city to city for years, ever seeking a point or purpose in each one. I could have been an autodidact peasant, now come to the city to show off his learning, pronounce a great theory of everything or a new path to spiritual enlightenment to rapt crowds in packed halls. Had I been younger, I could have been the eager naïf at the beginning of a cheap musical, ready to put his cases on the pavement, stand up, stretch his back, whistle through his teeth and sigh, *So, big city—whaddya got in store for me?*

I was, in truth, none of these things, yet also a little part of each of them.

But perhaps I should explain.

A FEW YEARS AGO, following the modest success of a book I had edited,[1] I was invited to give a series of lectures at a university in a small and somewhat remote city in central Europe which I shall not name. (There is no great reason for my reluctance to withhold the name of the city. Suffice to say that some of the incidents I will go on to relate, and the people mentioned in them, may want to maintain a veil of modesty. Those who know the city will no doubt recognise it; I trust their discretion.) A Professor at the city's well-established university had been much impressed by the book, and had contacted me about the possibility of delivering some lectures on the theme. After various proposals were entertained, I ended up being extended an invitation to give a series of ten lectures on lost, forgotten or unjustly neglected books (rather than lost, forgotten or unjustly neglected writers, which had been my previous field). Flattered by the invitation and the Professor's interest and enthusiasm, I jumped at the chance, especially seeing as the terms they were offering were more than generous. It was a good time to be leaving, as well. Endings—whether those of books or relationships—can make good beginnings.

---

[1] *The Biographical Dictionary of Literary Failure* (Melville House, 2014).

So that is why I found myself waiting at a station in a city whose name I could hardly pronounce, and where I did not speak a word of the local language, waiting for someone I would not recognise to take me somewhere I did not know.

This, I thought, this is good.

I WALKED ALONG THE station platform and ignored the stalls selling coffee, gigantic pastries and newspapers with disturbingly few vowels in their mastheads. I saw men dragging cases, a large family shouting at each other, commuters scuttling, two lovers breathlessly reunited. One or two uniformed drivers stood around smoking (yes, this was a place where it seemed you could still smoke in a railway station without fear of reproof), holding signs for hotels whose names I had seen in guides to the city. There were none for me, nothing with my name on it, the driver I had been promised apparently now long since departed due to the interminable delay. Obviously, there was the temptation to claim that I was Herr Vandervelde or Signor Bandera or Dr Flannery, not least to see how long I would be able to get away with the deception, but the temptation was brief. I am not a good actor, or liar. I get anxious too easily. I have a fear of being found out.

John Berger has written that "of all nineteenth-century buildings, the mainline railway station was the one in which the ancient sense of destiny was most fully re-inserted . . . in a railway station the impersonal and the intimate coexist. Destinies are played out." I waited to see what destiny would be played out for me, relishing my intimacy against the impersonality. In a French railway station, the hall immediately before the platforms is called *la salle des pas perdus*: the room of lost steps, a place which retains the echoes of the footfalls of those who crossed it and have long since vanished. As I waited there uncertainly, I wondered if they used the same expression in this country. I paced back and forth, losing steps, in an attempt to appear at least somewhat purposeful. If you have a purpose, I find, people are far more likely to ignore you.

After some time I remembered I had been wise enough to write the name and address of the hotel where I was to spend my first few evenings in the city on a slip of paper that I had stashed in my wallet. I found it folded between a few unfamiliar bank notes with improbably large numbers on them and decided I would walk out of the station, find the taxi rank, hand the paper to a driver and let myself be carried to my destination.

TAXI DRIVERS OCCUPY a unique place in the cultural imagination. They are, variously, dispensers of folk wisdom, intimates of the famous they have secretly ferried across the city by night, reliable guides to the best places to eat, potential fixers for a variety of scrapes or necessities, members of a secret society or metonymic representatives of a whole nation. I prefer to think of them as guides into the unknown: if you are patient, a taxi driver can take you anywhere you want to go, and you will never mind the price.

The best taxi drivers are the ones who do not speak, the ones who, with nothing more than a swift glimpse in the rearview wait for the precise mention of a destination, then look back to the road and begin to drive with a safe steady knowledge, hover just under the speed limit, throw an occasional tricksy shortcut when traffic ahead looms like bad weather, then safely deliver you, a click as the door releases, a smooth exchange of currency real or virtual, and then purr off again, already headed for their next cargo.

The taxi driver I chanced upon outside the station was not one of these people.

It was the orange football shirt that should have warned me (apart from the classic Dutch lineups of the '70s, orange is rarely a fortunate colour for teams), that and the crazed air of desperation he had as he opened the back door of his cab (a late '80s Lada or something approximating it) and half-shoved me in, chucking my suitcases in along with me. I handed him the paper, he squinted at it (yes, I worried about his eyesight) and then, with disturbing haste, hit the pedal.

Some people are born communicators, naturals who do not let the fact they share no language with their interlocutor block meaningful exchange.

This man was not one of these people, either.

As we screamed past the other drivers on the rank, his right hand jabbed over the back of his seat, its index finger extended into my face.

"You! You! Where you from?" I tried to reassure myself by thinking that he would know the streets so well as not to have to bother with the tedium of actually looking where he was going.

"England," I said.

"England! Number one country!" he shouted and moved to flip open the glove compartment, instantly disgorging tissues, cigarettes, street maps, breath mints and a flashlight before a tattered pocket dictionary fell onto the passenger seat and was then chucked in my direction. His gesture intimated that I should engage him in conversation by looking up every word I may have wanted to say. I closed the book and placed it deliberately on the suitcases piled on the seat beside me, but this did not deter his attempts to interact.

"Jan!" he shouted, and I wondered if he were saluting a friend he had noticed on the street, only to realise he was pointing at himself. "Jan! Jan!"

I told Jan I was very pleased to meet him and kindly requested that he keep his eyes on the road (hurriedly looking up "eyes" and "road" in the dictionary), but he did not seem to take my suggestion into account, narrowly missing a startled pedestrian as he continued his conversation.

"I you taxi now!" He laughed like a drain and I was curiously relieved to notice that he did have teeth. "My city!" he proclaimed with a majestic sweep of his arm, which prompted a swerve into the right-hand lane, the oncoming traffic squawking, disbanding, then re-forming behind us as we passed through.

We drove on, quite possibly in circles, though it was difficult to tell. The straight sweeping boulevard that led into the city centre from the station had road fractured into skittish alleyways and winding crescents flanked by tenement blocks. "Park!" shouted Jan as we passed an agglomeration of trees before hitting a narrow street which—though filled with pedestrians—apparently had permission for taxis to steam right through. "Shopping area!" shouted Jan, slicing his wing mirror against a kiosk serving something deeply fried and pungent. Intrigued as I was by my first glimpse of the new city, I tried not to look out of the window. Unfortunately, so did Jan.

His speed never slowed, not even as we took a tight corner to head down onto a modern slab of concrete that ran alongside a watercourse. "River!" We sank into a tunnel, my stomach arriving there a few seconds ahead of me before rapidly surfacing again. "Bridge!" The road fell away below me, the sound of rickety engine dispersing as we sped across the water, then veered left again, the road on this bank scarcely wider than the car we travelled in. "Old bridge!" I nodded, but it didn't stop. "Revolution Square!" he shouted as we passed along the edge of one large piazza, then looped, returning in the opposite direction while Jan shouted "Liberation Square!" The two squares seemed one and the same place, but by now I was well disoriented. While I have a good visual memory, I am not always good with a sense of direction.

The drive continued, thicker and faster: "Museum!" "Government!" "Theatre!" A rapid succession of attractions I scarcely had time to register before we sped past, halting only at one imposing edifice, which seemed to give Jan some trouble. His finger continued to point, jabbing back and forth, but no word came out. Eventually: "Building!" I nodded sagely.

His failure to name the building more accurately slowed him a little, and he took a turn to the pensive.

"You?" he said, still jabbing. "What you do here? Why you here?"

I thought about regaling him with the whole tale, or perhaps attempting to answer his question in a more existential fashion: *Why I here? Good question, Jan,* but decided to keep it simple and told him I was a writer, but he did not respond. I tried the dictionary, but, frustratingly, the word "writer" seemed to be absent from it.

"Here for work," I said, to still no response. "At the university." The final word seemed to register as he waved his hand back across the other side of the river, pointing into the distance.

"University!" There was a moment's silence and I worried I'd confused him as he slowed to a halt. "Writer?" he said, pointing at me. I nodded.

He got out of the car and beckoned me to follow. Gingerly, I followed him round to the back of the car where he began to open the boot. I wondered what I'd done. But then the boot opened, and it was clear what I'd done.

I never know quite how this happens, if there is some signal or scent I give off, some sign or aura I have attached to me that I believe invisible but which glows brightly for all others to see. Stacked in the trunk of Jan's car, in three soggy cardboard boxes, was a pile of old books. He waved his hand over them and grinned an all-too-familiar grin. The dealer showing his stash to his latest mark.

I looked at him glumly. I knew what I had to do. I bent over and started looking. The smell of damp woodiness, of promise, was inviting. The spines, too, peeling and faded perhaps, but always with that *something* which draws me in. I ran my fingers over some '70s school textbooks, a few tattered German paperbacks apparently left by tourists, a guide to skiing in the region, more textbooks, a couple of hefty tomes on anatomy that someone with more morbid taste might like to razor for their plates, but as I hit the second box, even soggier, the light had gone and I doubted I would find anything. It always happens in the first few titles; there's something there that if not perfect in itself, leads you on. But then, just as I was about to abandon the search, I noted a rare Ponç Puigdevall translation, and in the midst of a few yellow-spined Urania Italian science fiction pulps, a copy of *Black Lizards*, Max Long's little-known follow-up to his little-known *Burnt Island*. Jan looked at me, as though knowing he'd hooked me, but the truth was I was tired and already carrying too many heavy books. I hate to pass up an opportunity, but the Catalan writer interested me little and I already owned a copy of the Long.

Though I did wonder how this cabbie had chanced upon such things, attempting illumination was too much at this hour, so I stood up again, looked at Jan and shrugged. He shrugged too. Then we both shrugged again, and got back in the car.

~

IT WAS PROPERLY dark now, and I was losing faith that I would ever arrive anywhere when the cab stopped abruptly. "Hotel!" He pointed at a gloomy building squashed between two larger modern edifices, a faded sign above its door, its glitz long since departed.

I thanked him and handed him a note from my wallet as he dumped my cases onto the pavement, carefully placing the old dictionary on top.

"More fifty!" he said, indicating the book which I had inadvertently, it seemed, entered into a contract to purchase. I handed him another note and he pretended to find change with great difficulty. I couldn't be bothered, and waved my hand in the international gesture that I hoped meant "keep the change."

"Thank you!" he said, handing me a piece of paper with his name and an unfeasibly long phone number on it. "I Jan. I you taxi now! Remember . . ." He grimaced again, a tricky thought troubling his head before a sudden illumination, and then, in perfect English: "Only drink from lucky bottles!"

He smiled, then drove off into the gathering night at no less a pace than that at which we had arrived.

I WONDERED WHERE THIS Charon of the hire fleet had deposited me, but was relieved to see that the sign swinging outside the hotel bore the same word as the one scribbled on my paper: *Arosa*. Such a lovely name for such an unpromising place. I walked in, still dragging my cases, still suffering from the heat even though it was dark now and still wondering how to identify a lucky bottle from an unlucky one.

I was met by a tall man at the reception who gave me a curious look, a mixture of blankness and surprise, as if it were the strangest thing in the world that someone had walked into a hotel looking for a room, and yet that he must feign utter indifference. I wondered if perhaps he spoke no English, but when I repeated myself more loudly and slowly (a classic but usually doomed strategy), he looked at me with scrutiny and replied in perfect Received Pronunciation.

"Sir, I understand perfectly. The problem is that we have no idea who you are. You see, we *do* have a booking for a man with your name, but he was supposed to arrive last week. And anyway, he was German."

"And he never arrived?"

"No, sir."

"Then perhaps I could have his room."

"I'm afraid, sir, that things are rarely so simple."

~

ABOUT AN HOUR later, after several agitated telephone calls and having signed various forms claiming I had no idea what, I was handed a large brass key attached to a slab of wood the size of a small dining table and directed to a flight of stairs behind the now untroubled night clerk's desk.

Entering my room was also a procedure not without its complications. After managing to unlock the heavy lock with a satisfying clunk, I found I still could not open the door. I pushed for a good while until I noticed that the hinges were on the outside and that I had to pull rather than push to open the door toward me, as if I were entering a cupboard rather than a room.

~

I WONDER, NOW, looking back on it, if this tiny detail I have bothered to recount did not in some ways shape everything which was to happen over the next few months. I wonder if everything that happened to me and everything that I did were not in some ways shaped by the idea that I had come somewhere else—somewhere recognisable and yet so subtly different—such that when I entered that hotel cupboard, I had entered some kind of space which was both here, and not here.

As I say, it is only something I have occasionally surmised, and of which I could offer no proof, and yet the sense that I was somewhere *just not quite right* was one that took me over throughout my stay in the city—although at the time, I have to say, I hardly noticed it.

~

HAVING ENTERED, I could see why the door chose to open in such a fashion. The room was small, which would not have necessarily been a problem, but as well as its restricted size it was overwhelmingly stuffed with furniture, a lot of it, all exceedingly large. Chiefly, an enormous bed covered in a faded pink candlewick bedspread gave less than a few inches space around each side. At its foot sat a chair too large for one person and too small for two. A desk ran along one side of the room, but in contrast to the rest of the furnishings, the desk was but a plank deep and too shallow for even my smallest notebook.

But the room's most impressive feature wasn't the enormous bed or the tiny desk. Opposite the bed stood a wardrobe. I call it a wardrobe, I assumed it was a wardrobe, but it was more of a *presence*, another inhabitant of this small cupboard which was to be my home for the next few days. A black-lacquered mahogany behemoth that cleared the ceiling by less than an inch and must have been assembled in here, a cupboard within a cupboard. As I stared at it, disconcertingly seeing my reflection doing the same thing, I couldn't help thinking of the word "sarcophagus," though I couldn't quite think why. "Monolith" would have been a more appropriate word, its lucent black surface both reflecting and taking in all the scarce light the room had to offer. "Portal" might have been another word, but that would have been too literary a thought. I can't say I felt it watching me, but as I looked at it I realised I was watching myself.

Aware that I was having to step over my suitcases, I decided to open the cavernous wardrobe and store them in there. When I opened the door, however, I found that it was not empty. Inside hung six heavy overcoats, each one slightly different. One was of fine black cashmere, another of coarse brown wool, one was a vast thing with heavy satin lining, another a child's size. I wondered whom they were waiting for, these coats, or what kind of club or gang had left them there, and how long ago. I held one up and it smelt of camphor and soap powder, yet felt new, unworn.

I didn't put my cases in there, not wishing to disturb this strange absent family's quiet repose. Without undressing I lay on the bed, closed my eyes, then realised I would have to get up to turn out the light whose only switch was by the door. I thought that I should phone someone, call them to let them know I'd arrived safely, but then remembered I had no one to call. Arrival was unanchoring.

I wanted to read but was too tired to unpack. With the light still on, I fell asleep.

I APOLOGISE TO THE reader for including these seemingly trivial details, the dull and insignificant ephemera of any journey: train, station, taxi, hotel. Many of you will have had similar experiences, I don't doubt. And yet, before we move to the matter at hand, I think it worth pointing out that I believe nothing should go unnoticed, no matter how apparently trivial: sometimes, what may at first seem insignificant can turn out to be quite the opposite.

I was due to deliver my first lecture the very next day. Having tried the reader's patience for far too long already, I will at least spare you details of the usual anxiety dreams (suffice to say I found myself in a huge lecture theatre with old-fashioned banked wooden benches, ranks of students sitting there, all with no faces. I stood at a huge desk and in the manner of the nineteenth-century surgeon for whom the lecture theatre had been designed, began to perform a detailed autopsy on a hefty leather-bound tome, going at it with scalpel and saw, extracting its cartaceous viscera and holding them up delightedly before the awestruck crowd).

I woke early, dressed soberly in a black suit and white shirt and, being unsure of the weather, decided I should take my overcoat, just in case (I wondered if those left in the wardrobe had perhaps been furnished for my use, but none of them were particularly to my taste), and descended to the lobby where I was to meet the Profesora who was in turn to take me to the university and show me the lecture theatre.

The Profesora was to become a significant presence during my time in the city, so much so that I feel our first encounter should have had more moment than it did. Sitting in an armchair as though it were two and not eight in the morning, with a cigarette and a bowl of coffee so black it looked as though it would suck light into itself, this strange, angular woman rose from her chair like an Anglepoise lamp extending. She wore large sunglasses and a headscarf with a Mondrian pattern as geometrically angular as her body.

"Best morning, Doctor," she said. "Well arrived. We go now."

And go we did. She stubbed out her barely started cigarette and didn't stand as much as unfold. As she extended I saw her dress had the same motif as the headscarf, and in the act of walking her body assumed constant new perspectives as the patterns extended and shifted.

A younger woman who had been standing behind the Profesora, casually ignored and unintroduced, trailed us. I smiled at her; she returned the smile, but said nothing.

"Assistant," said the Profesora as we began to walk. I smiled again at Assistant; Assistant smiled back, but still said nothing.

The day was bright, the temperature brisk (the coat had not been a mistake) and the city streets clearer than they had been upon my arrival. Though autumn was in the air the day had the feel of spring. I felt almost optimistic as we crossed a bridge, headed through the winding streets of the old town and up to the imposing eighteenth-century university building. As we swept up its main staircase, the Profesora asked me what I was going to talk about this morning.

"I have no idea!" I said, and we all laughed. I am sure they thought I was joking. I wasn't.

I am far from being a meticulous planner, and prefer to leave things to chance, accident, trusting the spontaneity of the instant. I am not afraid to improvise, to follow the moment. I need to know who my audience is, to gauge their temperature, to see their faces, to feel their concerns before I can begin to talk to them on any meaningful level. The notes I keep are guides which may indicate the pathway without making me stick to it, fluid outline rather than rigid structure, suggestions not commands. Such is the best teaching, I feel.

As we wandered through a mile of corridors, the Profesora introducing me to various faculty members en route, I began to consider my options. I had my notebook with me, and decided that I would lecture on the book described on the page wherever my notes fell open. As we finally entered a low modern lecture room, a few curious faces looked up at me. I pulled out the notebook and stood behind the lectern. The book was marked with a ribbon, I noted, one which I did not remember having placed there. I tugged at it gently, and the book opened itself. Oh my, I thought. Really? Has fate dealt me this hand? And then, why not? A good hard one, a novel of infinite complexity and mystery. Yes, I thought, as the students filed in, opened their notebooks and began to hush, let us begin with this.

LECTURE NO. 1

Phrt by Christine Fizelle

Phrt, down from the stairway, onto the road, he waits and watches then walks with angular gait. Ja ja wunderbar the street sings as gasping gawps repeat and rally round. Plamp! Split splat splot! says Phrt, his waking words, angels still ringing in his ears, bright beams of summer in his winter head, this winter day, his feet cracking on the bold pavement, made of ice though not silver but gold in his dear wearyfolded but now new-waking world. Cold steps, ice steps thinks Phrt but he does not speak it for Phrt's words are away, asunder, awry, askew, not at one with this world, always at a tangent to those the Other Ones sound and scribble, his sounds, his marks so different from the language he knows but will not speak. No words for Phrt but his own! Ka faffle! he shouts as the Other Ones scrimble and scramble out of his path as he laughs and clears the street, his street, the only street in the world, made anew with every step he takes and every syllable he speaks. Sound and movement are creation thinks Phrt (in Phrt's way, if, should Phrt think at all, for who knows how or if or what Phrt thinks) as he steps, breathes, creating, sounding, singing Shmerk! Klmph! Zzaaattt!

It's an opening that is both utterly baffling and totally energising, not unlike the book which it opens: Christine Fizelle's *Phrt*. I could read this stuff for hours—and I warn the reader that there are hours of it—despite it being, I fully admit, largely incomprehensible. So why, I hear you ask, are you beginning a lecture course on great lost books with a book as difficult, impenetrable and almost wilfully obscure as this one? It is a good question, and one which I will attempt to answer.

Firstly: in a 1926 letter to Harriet Weaver, James Joyce wrote that "one great part of every human existence is passed in a state which cannot be rendered sensible by the use of wideawake language, cutanddry grammar and goahead plot." *Phrt* is a book which makes this clear—its language, while not perhaps dreamlike, does to me seem to belong to that strange realm of the half-awake, the moment when language fades and warps and befuddles itself, that moment when things have a different kind of clarity. This leads on to my second point.

Every book is an attempt to create a world. Dickens built a London, Faulkner and Flannery O'Connor a U.S. South, the Brontës fashioned their Northern gothic moorlands, the aforementioned Joyce remade Dublin then took it apart again, and who can see Prague without Kafka? In her way, Fizelle does the same thing, but it is not a city that her book creates: the difference with *Phrt* is that it is a book which attempted to create a world within another world, a world that already did not exist.

Again, I see your questioning faces, but patience. Let me explain.

Christine Fizelle was born in 1912 in Sandymount, Dublin, then as now an affluent suburb of the Irish capital. Almost a coeval of Samuel Beckett, she shares more than a city with him (and despite no evidence to prove it, one cannot help but wonder if they ever met, as children perhaps, playing by the sea somewhere, weighing pebbles in their mouths). She didn't spend long in Dublin, however; her father was a diplomat, at first in service of the then British

Empire, but having managed to keep his powder dry he moved seamlessly into the administration of the Irish Free State abroad. As the ambassador's daughter, Fizelle spent much of her young life living out of a suitcase (or, more probably, a well-built trunk) as the family hauled their way from Ottawa to London to Paris to Warsaw to Belgrade. She was a girl who must have heard shards of many different languages, and felt at home in none of them. Accounts describe her as bright but reclusive, often only appearing at formal dinners to give a brief piano recital before scurrying away again. It seems strange that on reaching her majority she did not return to Ireland or Britain to study, but—perhaps because of her father's famously domineering character (admirably described in F. X. Mulligan's biography *Fizelle's Fortunes*)[2]—seemed unable or unwilling to break free of the family bonds. Marriage was proposed to her on a few occasions (a seemingly potential opportunity for escape) but she refused every offer—perhaps because each such proposal had been carefully brokered by her father.

She weathered the Second World War in Belgrade before moving to West Berlin following her father's death in 1948. After this her trail vanishes, though accounts suggest she may have been in Helsinki, Ibiza and New York during the fifties and sixties. Nothing was ever heard of her again.

She was, I believe, a person who never found herself at home, and revelled in this. Being not-at-home, being *unheimlich* one could say, is perhaps an essential prerequisite for a writer, being out of your skin, neither here nor there. This puts one at a terrible risk of isolation and loneliness but at the same time offers an incredible freedom, that of always being a foreigner, always being other. This is something which is central to an understanding of *Phrt*, as we shall see.

---

[2] Molloy and Malone, 1954.

What we do know for certain about Fizelle is that she was always a passionate follower of the avant-garde. Mulligan's aforementioned biography of her father mentions the rages he would fly into when the young Christine returned late from some *salon* or other, perhaps trailing a long-haired poet or experimental filmmaker. She was forbidden from giving any more of her piano recitals when one evening, instead of dutifully performing Schubert lieder, she chose to play some Schoenberg and then started in on Satie's *Vexations*.

And this is what is important about Fizelle. Her travels around Europe had forged her character in Dadaism, surrealism, futurism, imagism and lettrism. From the little we know of her, we can see that she dreamed a world in which Joyce, Tzara, Stein, Pound, Marinetti, Carrington, Breton and their ilk were the norm, the standard, the average, the writers whose works bored schoolchildren and whose titles, embossed in gold on cheap paperbacks, filled railway and airport bookstalls or were left piled in junk shops and on streetside stalls, a world in which it was *these* writers whom even those strange people who never read books might occasionally peruse. Christine Fizelle's world was one in which dodecaphonic serialism filled the pop charts and the dance floors (dance floors where the hottest dancers would break out their Merce Cunningham, Twyla Tharp or Pina Bausch moves), where Maya Deren was Disney and Antonin Artaud a Broadway smash. This was the world Fizelle imagined, and—in her head—lived in.

And then—out of artistic bravery or sheer madness, I'll leave you to decide—she decided to write a novel that would be experimental, to a degree that would be difficult *in that world*.

She was, of course, doomed to failure even before she started, yet her attempt was a more than valiant one, and *Phrt*, the book which represented that attempt, is, I would argue, a testament to all that is brave and good and right for those who have long toiled in literature's Research and Development department for scant reward.

So what *is* this book? A conventional reading of *Phrt* (if one can hazard a "conventional" reading of such a complex work) would have it that it is the story of a deeply eccentric man, Phrt, whose baffled attempts to make his way through a world stifled by convention end in his undoing. This is all true but seems a woefully inadequate description of the book.

Phrt, like many books of its ilk, belies its reputation for difficulty. I believe it is nowhere near as extreme or obscure as it is reputed to be. Partly this is because it moves itself along on that singsong prose, and if readers let themselves be carried along, a clear story emerges: Phrt is a character, a man and also little more than a breath of air. His world is that which he creates himself, his struggle to live in a world that is not his, a world that he has not brought into being, and his way of attempting to do this is simply to ignore the other world altogether. We never quite inhabit Phrt, who is not a man as much as a collection of snorts and squeaks and sounds, glyphs and marks on the page, yet is also someone who does in some sense breathe. Fizelle moves us close to him then away again, with a careful indirect prose so that we are with Phrt halfway, able to see his world and also the one around him, one closer to ours. The book, in the end, not only creates its own world, it creates many.

~

The few critics who have occupied themselves with the book diverge, but for me, this book is all about language itself. Phrt speaks entirely in his own made-up words, his dialogue consisting of phots, shmirms, quizzles, franges and blats. Wittgenstein, of course, points out that no language can ever be entirely private, and some critics have claimed that the book is to some degree an attempt to counter Wittgenstein's idea. I would disagree.

Taking the book on its own terms, there are two reasons for this. Firstly, Phrt does not even think of his utterances as a language, but more as a way of bringing the world into being. Secondly, and perhaps more importantly, it is the impossibility of this that leads to his downfall.

What I would argue, conversely, is that *Phrt* does not attempt to represent human consciousness in any way, but to reconfigure it through writing. A huge task, of course, but always one worth attempting. The attempt is always brave and always fraught. One of *Phrt*'s most famously difficult passages consists of eight pages that are purely typographical symbols (most readers, perhaps wisely, skip through this part. Looks pretty—but how the hell are you supposed to read it?), yet we can again see that it questions the relationship between sound and the marks we make on paper, the very basis of writing.

The book focuses on and problematizes the relationship of writing to sound, of consciousness to meaning. And from this apparently abstract concept it tries to work out the whole wider question of what it means to be in the world, of what it means to exist.

There are two key moments in this huge book. The first comes just after a quarter of the way through when, as far as I understand, Phrt, on one of his daily walks around the city, sees someone who looks exactly like him. At first there is silence, a block (represented by a sentence that stops partway through, then four totally blank pages, followed by a resumption of the sentence), after which there occurs a strange mirroring: exactly the same text (clearly recognisable as one of Phrt's speeches due to its pure agglomeration of sprts, phzs, hounzels, whikes and shrvles) is printed side-by-side on facing pages of the book. This goes on for ten pages. What may look like a printer's or binder's error is actually Fizelle re-enacting what happens as Phrt meets this character. I confess I cannot fathom who it is—a brother, sister, twin? A look-alike or double? Or merely some other kind of kindred spirit? Whoever it is, Phrt has found someone else who shares his language, and he can do nothing about it other than replicate theirs.

The second key point is significant in that it is only when Phrt utters something vaguely recognisable that his end begins. Apparently incensed by some intrusion into his day or some perceived petty slight against his person, he stands in the main square of the city and loudly shouts "Shitcoat mangrate!" He is promptly arrested by two uniformed guards, thrown into prison, then hauled up before a judge. It seems that his exasperated phrase has been taken as a slanderous slur on the country's president— Phrt's straying into some kind of meaning has caused his undoing.

~

So why did this book disappear? Why is it not cited in lists of great adventurous, difficult and challenging writing? Why is it not mentioned in the same breath as *Finnegans Wake*?

There are several reasons for this, all of them, I fear, crushingly obvious and banal. The first is sheer brute bad luck. The book was not a complete failure: it was published by John Calder in 1961 (following on from many other fine books, such as Dola de Jong's *The Tree and the Vine* and Gerhart Hauptmann's *The Heretic of Soana*, for example) but it sold little, was reviewed only in the Cleveland *Plain Dealer* (the review was not favourable) and soon sank with little trace. The book rapidly went out of print and (as far as I know), there were no other works, and no chance for Fizelle to promote her back catalogue, as she herself seems to have chosen to disappear just around the time the book came out.

There is another important fact I should perhaps mention here. If you have not had the pleasure of coming across this book before, I should warn you that it is a big one: the Calder edition runs to six hundred and forty-five pages. The spine breaks, the pages fall out. Added to which, many of those six hundred and forty-five pages are, as I have already pointed out, if not entirely incomprehensible, then certainly difficult to penetrate. This alone need not be a hindrance; other such works exist. However, remember, this is a huge, complex work by a *female* writer. What other great work—and yes, for we still have this terrible habit of equating length with worthiness—is there by a female writer that is of this length? Women, it seems, are still allotted the slight, the small, the personal, the domestic. But the epic is for men. (There is, of course, *The Tale of Genji* and George Eliot, and Sigrid Undset wrote a massive book, but carefully divided it into separate volumes. But the only equivalent I can think of is Goliarda Sapienza's almost equally neglected *L'arte della gioia*.) I wonder if this, too, is not one of the reasons Fizelle has never been granted her rightful recognition.

~

While I have described the prose as joyous, and most of it is, the book does contain its darker, more violent moments—most notably the long passages in which Phrt moves into capitals *HHAAMMSSCHH!! GGGRRRAAATTT!! SCCHWWIINKKK!!!* or goes into endless lowercase grumbles *schammmtekwak schmmamble stttakke, fffiddring falding mambling scchmmatt*. Some critics have taken these as intimations of suicide, of death at his own hand, or that of one of the many who he is, of how his unstable, unfixed self will tip itself over into something else. As may be expected, the ending of the book is ambiguous, but it seems that Phrt ceases to exist as his language evaporates from around him with an endless exhalation of breath. So let us leave him there, thank you Fizelle, thank you Phrt.

Phhrrrrrr. Scchhhhmmmummpppp. Hhhhhhhhhhhhhh.

As I concluded, I was momentarily taken aback when a number of students used their knuckles to rap furiously on the wooden desks, creating a most disconcerting sound, but on seeing my bafflement the Profesora (whom, if you remember, we have already briefly met) approached.

"Worry not. It is good thing when they make this noise." I sighed relief and smiled at the now-departing audience. "Come," continued the Profesora. "Now we lunch." I didn't even have to assent to her suggestion (if indeed it was a suggestion), as she merely led the way.

I had imagined a bustling canteen, being seated at a long table surrounded by the eager chatter of knowledge-hungry youth, or perhaps a little trattoria or bistro-type place frequented by academics, small glasses of red with a long lunch over discussion of publications and conferences and gossip filled with barely concealed bitterness. It was to be neither. Lunch was to be consumed in the Profesora's office, and lunch was to consist of black coffee and cigarettes.

"It is safer here," she said, locking the door behind her.

~

But before I continue, I should fill in some details for the no doubt curious reader.

Following my initial invitation from the Professor at the

university, I had been handed over to his colleague (who always signed herself "Profesora," boldly ignoring any internationalisation of her title) for the dull-but-necessary details. And so it was that the Profesora had offered to meet and accompany me on that first morning. Even though she had given no description of herself (and the rudimentary faculty website contained nothing so vulgar as a photograph), I knew upon descending to the hotel lobby that morning that this woman of knees, elbows, chin and cheekbones had to be her. My suspicions were immediately confirmed by that unusual greeting: *Best morning! Well arrived!* The Profesora's tangential relationship to the English language was one to which I would become accustomed over the weeks that followed, and—I have to say—would soon begin to appreciate. Looking back, I suspect it was not a linguistic weakness on her part (as I initially assumed), but rather an attempt to give her speech a richer character, a language formed out of her first language, meeting her second one halfway, or rather, crash-landing in its midst.

We were not, however, alone for lunch, but joined by the ever-present and still-unnamed Assistant. Seeing as she will play a certain part in this tale, allow me a moment to describe her: no less striking than the Profesora but considerably less angular, this woman had a tangle of black hair, radically cropped at the edges and with a severe fringe. Her clothing was equally austere: a starched white shirt with a Peter Pan collar buttoned right up and a tightly fitted black cotton blazer, a look either extremely modish or simply unchanged in fifty years or more. It made her look as though she were a student at the Bauhaus in the late '20s, a radical Dadaist, vorticist, imagist or some kind of -ist. For all I knew, or would ever know, perhaps she was.

~

AND SO IT was that I sat with this pair, in a large and well-lit yet strangely gloomy university office (the bare walls, I think, the dead plants), over a lunch that consisted of nothing but coffee and cigarettes, having my performance casually eviscerated.

I myself had been reasonably pleased with the outcome. The lecture theatre had been brim-full, some attendees even sitting on the steps, and only a few of them had walked out, after all. Most students had done the banging on the desks thing. Fizelle had had her say, her *Phrt* had breathed again: this was important to me, and I had at least had the pleasure of reading some of her addictive prose aloud and at a notable volume.

The Profesora did not share my opinion.

"What happened at the end?" she asked. "Were you having a cough explosion?"

"No," I protested. "That's how the book ends—I was ending the lecture with the ending of the book." I had believed it a good tie-up, a solid conclusion, a fitting finish. The Profesora disagreed.

"No. It does not end with cough explosion, more . . . gentle breeze."

"Do you know the book?"

"Of course. Very dull. Terrible dry. I do not know why you chose it at all, not least for your virgin lecture." I was, I admit, taken aback by the fact that she knew the book, but I shouldn't have been. Up until this point, I had regarded myself as one in a field of one, often pondering over books no one else knew even the existence of. I should have known better. This was a university, after all, which held chairs in both Pseudo and

Crypto Bibliography and had its own department of 'Pata-physics.

"Some students, though, knocked on their desks. Is that not a good thing?"

"We are polite people. And, how can I set this? Some of our students are . . . not so clever." As the Assistant filled the Profe-sora's basin-sized cup with more coffee, my interlocutor warmed to her theme. "You have an engaging style, Doctor, but please. Not so friendly. We are polite people, but not friendly people. We do not appreciate friendly."

"Less friendly?"

"Less friendly." She lit another cigarette. "And more quo-tations please. Let us *feel* the book. And nothing so difficult, please. Nor so long. And spare us the pot biography. A writer's life has nothing to do with their work."

"Contentious."

"Who? Me?"

"Your statement, rather."

"You may say so, and I may ignore you. Your lecture was *literary criticism* or something." I suggested that I had been in-vited here for the express purpose of literary criticism, but she disagreed. "Oh no. Not literary critic. People can read all that dullness in books, should they want. You should try and *enter-tain* more."

"So I should be more entertaining, and less friendly."

"Precise."

I turned to the Assistant in search of help. She smiled again but still did not speak, though this time at least, the smile grew wider, revealing a disturbingly sharp set of teeth.

"And all that matter about Wittgenstein," continued the Profe-sora. "Please no more of old Ludwig. We are enough with Ludwig here." More coffee. "And . . ." More cigarettes. "And . . ." It went on. "And . . ." I am afraid I cannot remember her full catalogue of complaint, only that it seemed to last longer than a dream in which one is trapped. I came round at the mention of the Professor.

"He sends his regrets. He was not able to be present today. This is perhaps good." She leaned in. "Things at the university are, I must say, in a difficult phase at the moment. I shall tell more of this later."

I glanced at the Assistant. The Assistant glanced back, this time with a finely arched eyebrow.

"Lunch is finished. We have work, Doctor! Onward!" She opened the door and gestured me out. "We will see us presently. In the mean, don't go looking for a three-legged dog!"

I SPENT MUCH OF the next week in a state of pleasant aim-lessness. The days kept their warmth, though the shadows lengthened by late afternoon. The combination of autumn light, summer haze and blasts of approaching winter tilted every-thing, threw perspective into the odd. Or, at least, this is what I told myself on my ever-longer walks around the city. I had only seen the place from the window of a speeding taxi or by trying to keep up with the Profesora and her assistant. I had now de-cided to find the place properly, by walking it.

I had no map, no guidebook. Though I love both of those things, I find them useless in the field. I prefer to read guide-books as works of fiction, describing distant places I know I shall never visit. I prefer to look at maps as works of art, admiring the grace of contour lines and endless rivers, the counterpoint of place names and feature symbols. Both, I find, are disappoint-ments in reality.

Having no guide other than my senses helps with my pre-ferred method, the *dérive*, the wander away from the main bou-levards trafficking me into their commerce, and off into side streets, down alleyways, up steps, across bridges.

The city was a succession of flights and drops, a sequence of the right throbs and the wrong. Bridges old and new gave out onto small squares, four-lane highways or sometimes sim-ple dead ends. Some streets thronged with pedestrians, then emptied suddenly as if a signal I had failed to understand had been given. Parks were plentiful, still filled with deep green conifers waiting for the winter. Benches welcomed the weary backside of the wanderer. Drunks joined me, offering a share of their silent bottles.

The people did indeed seem to be polite but not friendly, and this reassured me. I am not a man to enter into casual conversation lightly and was relieved to find there seemed to be no expectation of this custom here. Being unobliged to make awkward conversation with strangers freed me to become invisible, drift, watch the gentle crowds, noting how strangely familiar they sometimes seemed. One of the recollections I had from the lecture was how some of the faces in the crowd had seemed familiar. This was impossible of course, but I took to believing that perhaps it had to do with age and the passing of time. Everyone now, I thought, looked like someone else. There was always some visual trace, some connection I could make between a new person and one I had met or known somewhere before. I'd seen the face of someone I'd once spent a frantic New Year's Eve with and never seen again, a former schoolteacher, and—in one girl—the face of someone I never wanted to see again.

Such were the kinds of thoughts that meandered through my mind as I too meandered through the city on one of those long days.

I came upon a café, the perfect place, large wooden tables and a checkerboard floor, a zinc-topped bar backed by mirrored shelves on which were stacked an impressive range of bottles. It seemed to have no name, only a sign bearing a question mark hanging above the door. I found a table by the window and subsequently spent many hours there, alongside a coffee, or something stronger, a couple of books, my thoughts.

Looking back, I think of those days as some of my happiest in the city. The sting of the Profesora's critique had soon worn away: I'd had worse reviews in my time, after all. It also made me think I couldn't very well bugger up next week's lecture much more. I let the thought of it hang around at the back of my mind as I wandered, sat or drank, occasionally writing down inspirations or ideas in the notebook I kept in my coat pocket, but was careful not to let the thought of it bother me unduly, confident something would take shape and form. I had enough books to talk about, after all.

Having cut ties with any notion of home helped. No plants dying, no cat to feed. No one to call. Everything I had was with me. The only thing that gave me unease was the hotel room and its strange claustrophobia. I own I spent much of the day out walking to avoid the place, but consoled myself with the thought that I would not be there much longer, and would soon have an apartment in which to pass the days which I knew would soon grow colder.

One of these days, the light going and the ? café emptying, I paid the extremely reasonable bill then decided to try an alternative route back to the hotel, perhaps only to prolong my absence from it. It turned out, however, that the café was actually located almost directly behind the hotel, and I merely needed to turn a corner and there I was, back. Such was the disorienting geometry of this place, the foreshortening of perspective, or perhaps merely my own poor sense of direction. This city was forever shifting.

~

THE ARRIVAL BACK at the hotel held another surprise. I had a visitor.

"I come with news," said the Assistant. I was surprised to hear her speak, having blithely assumed that perhaps she couldn't. I asked her what news she had to bring, and if she would like to join me for a cup of tea in the hotel lobby.

"No, there is no tea here," she informed me, and I do not doubt she was right. The lobby was but a small anteroom, largely taken up by the absent concierge's desk and two stiff-backed comfortless chairs.

"Ah, no, I suppose not. So let's have news, instead."

"Your apartment, I'm afraid, is still not ready. There are some problems, nothing serious, but it does mean you will have to spend a few more days here." I concealed my disappointment, because that's what I do. "If it is any consolation, the Profesora would like to invite you for dinner one night. She hopes the Professor can come as well."

"That would be lovely."

"She will be in contact."

"Excellent." News delivered, the Assistant stood there, looking at me. I smiled at her; she didn't smile back.

"You're here for Guyavitch, too, aren't you?" she said.

And she was right.

I HAVE BEEN remiss, I admit. I have been hiding some of my own truth, though this has been for the simple expedience of narrative economy rather than any intent to deceive. While everything I have so far recounted about my invitation to the university, the circumstances of my arrival in the city, the delivery of the first lecture and so on and so on is true, I did have an ulterior motive for coming to this place.

Since editing *The Biographical Dictionary* I had become more and more acquainted with further stories of vanishing writers and obscure manuscripts. It turned out that my research had barely scratched the surface of a world teeming with obsessives and dedicates. Some were scholars, others cranks, a few downright dangerous. I constantly received (and continue to receive) emails, letters, missives, articles and manuscripts as well as the occasional threat. Some of them were, I have to admit, more interesting and promising than others, and as stories unfolded I often found myself (despite my better judgment) chasing leads and following trails, attempting to weave together threads that often only tangled or unravelled. Some of these stories I may have space to recount later, but there was one writer who fascinated me. His name was Maxim Guyavitch.

Little is known about Guyavitch, and the little we do know is far from certain. He may have been born somewhere in Austria-Hungary around 1880—some claim he was Moravian, others Dalmatian. Some claim he was an orphan who joined the army in order to save himself, others that he was the only son of a neglectful bourgeois family, others that he never really existed at all but was merely the pseudonym of someone who had a far more respectable career. There is, needless to say, no basis for any of these theories save for that they are derived from stories which appear in his writings, and his writings are few: Guyavitch only ever wrote nine short stories.

All great works of literature, Walter Benjamin wrote, either invent a genre or dissolve one. Guyavitch, in the tiny space of those stories, did both. It is my firm conviction that were he better known he would rival Kafka in the literary imagination, supplant Joyce for the quantity of critical scholarship, challenge Gogol to ownership of the overcoat.

The only thing all the people I had read or corresponded with could agree on was that Guyavitch had been laid to rest in this very city. So, my motives for coming here? The handsomely remunerated lectures, of course, the fact that the Professor here was an authority on the shadowy author, but also, I admit, to make my own small pilgrimage, to visit the man's obscure grave.

"Do you know where I may find it?" I asked the Assistant.

"I think so," she replied, "though things are sometimes not so easy to find here."

~

BUT MORE OF this later. A week has almost elapsed and it is now time to deliver my second lecture. Be with me, dear reader, as I awake late and flustered (poor sleep due to anxiety dreams again, which I shall not trouble you with save to tell you they involved putting a book through a fine sieve in order to find what would be left of it), begin to run to the university only to find Jan the taxi driver en route.

"Bok!" shouts Jan, then "Ahoj! Sdravo! Witam! Sveiki!," his effervescent greeting apparently running the gamut of the languages he seems barely familiar with, as he loads me into his cab and speeds up the hill with little regard for his gearbox or human life before neatly off-loading me in front of the main steps of the lecture hall. I clutch the notebook and battered paperback in my pocket as if charms, enter, and take a deep breath.

Sweeter Than the Milk of River Toads in the Mating Season by Gabriel Ferreira

Had I known the madness my book would cause, the violence, the passion, the death, I would have written it anyway. Had I even had the chance to change, it would have been more than I could have done. Our ends are inscribed in our beginnings. Our destinies are not ours to play with: I was guided by a greater hand. Let this be my testament: I did everything for love.

It's a striking opening to a striking book. A grand statement, a declaration of intent and an unapologetic staking out of the novel's narrative territory.

Sweeter Than the Milk of River Toads in the Mating Season, Gabriel Ferreira's first and only novel, is narrated by Peter Ratzlaff, a callow but earnest Mennonite missionary who, together with his brother Thomas, sets off into the interior of an unnamed South American country with the dream of bringing the word of the Lord to the people who live there. Though the brothers were born and raised in the country, they rapidly find themselves in a land that is very strange to them, one whose climate, customs and landscape they are ill-equipped to navigate. Even as their journey becomes more arduous, they insist on wearing their traditional costume, eating the dull, hard rations they have brought with them rather than the local food, speaking Plautdietsch as far as possible (which isn't very far, and gives rise to some notable comic interludes at the beginning of the book—their attempts to order chicken to eat in a hostelry, for example), and on maintaining their modest, godly behaviour.

As they travel farther into the "green hell," Peter notices how he and his brother slowly begin to change. At first it is almost imperceptible, nothing more than leaving some of their buttons undone, or finding delicious the rich green leaves of the plants whose names they do not know and which they had previously thought revolting, hardly even food worthy of animals. They both begin to revel in the landscape they had until now found barbaric: taking joy in the plumage of strange birds, the deep colours of the flowers with their intoxicant perfumes, the shrill cries of the monkeys who leap around them, thrilled by the danger of the snakes they see uncoil from trees, the glimpse of a panther's coat through the dense foliage.

It's an outsider's fantasy of course, and although the men are native to the country, they view its interior with an almost Orientalist eye. The story may, at this point, indeed seem one already told, but bear with us, for there is far further to travel yet. The narrator's enraptured but occasionally trite prose for example, is something which, in an act of intriguing authorial self-reflexivity, he begins to examine:

> The heart of the country, I wrote in my notebook, not disappoint-
> ed in my choice of obvious words, for this really was the heart of
> the country. I was not merely reliant on an over-used figure of
> speech but I felt I could feel the very land around me beating,
> pulsating, pumping, feel the energy in the streams which ran past
> us and the water which poured from the leaves, livid red blood

the colour of the spiders and flowers. This land was alive, and I
was close to the vital core of life itself, its pulsing centre.

~

Eventually, they find this core, and the people who live there. There
is no heart of darkness here though, quite the opposite: the tribe
they encounter seem the happiest people they can imagine. *Surely*
they had already heard the word of the Lord, and they were now living
in its bliss. There have been warnings: the brothers had been told not
to even attempt to convert this tribe. The people there, they had
been told, were the wastrels of the forests, its vagabonds, its idlers.
The men, it was said, were feckless and lazy, the women wanton, the
children neglected. They were known for hunting as little as possible,
finding just enough to sustain themselves and spending the rest of
their time slinging their hammocks between the trees or engaging
in more reckless pursuits.

But here, the brothers begin to diverge: Peter finds himself
ever more intrigued by them but Thomas soon has a crisis of faith,
rebuttons his tunic and strides away into the jungle.

It is the "idle pursuits" that have done for them: Peter is drawn
in, while Thomas is disgusted by the way the natives act. It is not,
however, what it may seem, nor what the reader (in this so far, so
predictable book) may have anticipated. Although the tribe are
friends with the coca leaf, mescal, ayahuasca, yagé, the titular milk
of river toads in the mating season, marijuana, peyote and *Salvia*
divinorum, none of these are as potent for them as the power of a
story.

This tribe are storytellers, and stories are their drugs. For them,
stories are not mental escapades, but are lived, richly, fully, viscerally.
Every person in the tribe, man, woman and child, has the power:
once they begin to recount, the others fall into trances. There are

some figures, elders of the tribe, the Tellers, whose power to do this is even stronger. The most potent of their stories are not allowed to minors, although minors, as they will, often do their damnedest to hear them, and sometimes succeed. Unusually, apart from their creation myth, there is no canon, and stories beget stories, in endless circulation, endless supply, one folding into another and generating a third, fourth, fifth, the characters always recognisable but always changing. Every story is told anew, nothing is ever repeated. And the fount of all these stories is that creation myth: a leopard, drunk on the milk of the river toad, brought the world into being with a story, and will end it again when the story finishes.

There is only one sin in their world: writing. It seems the concept of writing is not one that has arrived here, though in a conversation with one of the Tellers, Thomas and Peter hear a story—that writing has been known, and it has been banished from their world, never to be spoken of again. To write one of their stories would be simultaneously to kill it and to give it a power stronger and more dangerous than it ever should have.

Thomas feels the Devil at work, and—as mentioned—leaves, heading off, perhaps never to be seen again. Peter, on the other hand, is entranced. Here he feels the word of the Lord manifested, made flesh, and though the stories these people tell are different from the ones he has learned, those stories of saints and sages in far-off desert lands come home to him, here: in the heart of the country he has found the Bible of the Forest. And this is his inspiration, his reverse vocation: he knows what he has to do—he has to take the word back to the city. And to do that, he has to break the tribe's only law.

So far, so magically realist. We've got the measure of the book by now: taking after Márquez, yet with healthy injections of Cortázar, Borges and Ocampo, making for a curious and often uneasy mix of those traditions, both lush and populist, yet maintaining a certain underlying intellectual and logical rigour.

Yet the next section of the book is radically different, almost a different novel, although still one with its distinctive tropes. Instead of the overheated magical realism of the opening section, we are now with the starving writer/big city/garret trope. Peter is back in the city, now having renounced his vocation and his faith, apparently in the grip of some delirium. He has no money, is constantly feverish, and always writing down a story, one from the hundreds he heard in the jungle, but he cannot find its form: this story will not fit onto paper. The story constantly appears as if in his peripheral vision, then slips away again, as elusive as one of the creatures he saw in the shadows of the jungle. He has filled thousands of pages, which now litter the flyblown apartment where he finds himself, the top floor of a tenement, the rest of which seems to be a brothel. He passes his days and nights feverishly, furiously writing, but he can find neither the beginning nor the end of his tale. It is ever evanescent, always escaping from him. His only distraction comes from the girls downstairs who occasionally visit (the descriptions jar a little on the modern ear; the book is very much of its time in so many ways); one asks if she can read what he has written, and for a long time he will not let them, then in a fit of despair permits them. The girls begin to visit ever more frequently, always wanting more. Peter convinces himself that this is love, and that he is writing for love, that love is the heart of the word of the Lord, and love is the thing that will tell his story.

The women talk to their clients, one of whom is a publisher, curious to know about this strange tale which has so enraptured them. He ventures upstairs, and rapidly finds himself, also, addicted.

To part three, and again it seems we are reading yet another novel. The focus moves on a few years in time and out, a wide angle, a panorama of the whole country, a country now in chaos, on the brink of collapse. But it is not financial collapse, economic ruin, corruption, warfare or a natural disaster that has caused this: it is Peter's book. The devious publisher, inevitably, took parts of it and put it out, not knowing what he was doing: releasing into the world a strain of narrative so pure that it has become a drug. People cannot get enough of it, people are quitting their jobs to stay home and read, public services have been all but abandoned, everyone wants more. Original copies have rocketed in price, now only available to those in the know, for wheelbarrows of hard cash. Pirates have started pushing out cheap variants, but these have only left the addicted ill and wanting more of the pure stuff, the good stuff. Some are selling in instalments, only one chapter, then a page, then a line at a time to ever more desperate people. Publishers rapidly become gangs, cruising around the city in dark-windowed bulletproofed cars, armed bodyguards at their flanks, their imprints now the sigla of private militias, "book fairs" are a cover for clan summits, likely as not to end in bloodbaths.

And yet, despite the darkness, the book here returns to some of its original lush extravagance of tone. The chaos is carnivalesque, rapturously described, a tropicalia fever dream, soundtracked by Os Mutantes.

Eventually the government of the country, corrupt and corrupted as they have been, are forced to do something. Their North American neighbours have heard that a translation is in the works (a collaboration of publishing gangs), and that the contagion will spill. Yet when it turns out the publishing cartels have all too friendly relations with the government, a coup ensues. A military junta is installed, presided over by The General, who despite his large moustache and permanent dark glasses, Peter recognises as Thomas, his long-jungle-lost brother.

Peter begins work on a second book, one which this time he claims will act as an antidote to his first, a book that will set him— and the rest of the country—free from their addiction. The General, however, does not approve of this: Peter's liberating work is banned, and anyone found reading it sent to a distant prison.

The plot is mechanical, inevitable yet unpredictable as a good plot should be. The climax is truly surprising, and for once I shall not spoil it for you. Suffice to say that given the occasionally clunky mechanics of the plot, this is a story that does not end—if it ends at all—in the way that its exposition may have led us.

Given the immense popularity of this type of fiction around the world, we have to ask our question: Why then has this book been lost?

Sweeter Than the Milk of River Toads in the Mating Season was first published in 1970, in Paraguay. While outsiders may see it as forming a part of the tradition of South American literature, indeed, a rare Paraguayan voice in that canon, in its native country it was seen as something very different. Paraguay at the time was under the military rule of General Alfredo Stroessner, a man sometimes known as "the bastard's bastard," a man so uniquely unpleasant the likes of Pinochet, Papa Doc and Trujillo could only look up to him. Needless to say, it was both brave and perhaps reckless of Ferreira to publish a book with a character called "The General." Nevertheless, published it was (by a small cooperative of independent publishers, all of whom were soon "disappeared" after the work hit the streets) and rapidly became a great word-of-mouth success (needless to say, none of the official newspapers ever dared review such a work), selling out its original print run in weeks, then being republished in various pirated and samizdat editions. The Department of Internal Security (the polite name for the intensely feared secret police) got to work rapidly, and it is thought that almost every copy of the book, official and unofficial, was destroyed in the few years following its publication. Even though Paraguay is now a functioning liberal democracy, the book is still barely spoken of. It is as if the horrors it provoked have left too great a trauma.

Others claim the reason is more simple: its satire is too blunt, Ferreira's style a too-obvious copy of Márquez, which lacks the depth of Vargas Llosa or the playful finesse of Cortázar. That high strain of magic realism is no longer the fashion it was, perhaps the more stringent prose of Hilst, Lispector, Pizarnik or Rulfo having become more prominent.

Ferreira himself, allegedly still alive in the United States under an assumed name with a retinue of bodyguards, has never written another book. Like his character, he has been unable to publish a book that will set him free from his first one.

Thank you.

A N APPRECIATIVE MURMUR arose in the lecture theatre, accompanied by the rumble of desks being thumped, then slowly died away as the crowd filed out. And glancing down at my tattered copy of *Sweeter Than the Milk*, I fell to remembering the summer I had discovered Ferreira.

I'd been going out with a six-foot-two, redheaded Slovenian performance artist with a tattooed elbow, but the relationship had begun to sour when her Pekinese bit my finger, leading to an extremely unpleasant septic reaction, and when she eventually left, taking Fernando (the dog) with her, I can't say I was too sorry, especially as it then left me more time to get on with my research into Paraguayan magic realism (an admittedly small field). Talking about the book brought her back to me, and though I could picture her perfectly, I found I had no recollection whatsoever of her name. I sat looking at the dull walls around me, trying to drag it up from somewhere, but no, nothing came.

I instead fell to contemplating my more present circumstances. I have often wondered if there is not some Platonic ideal, some essential form or some wisdom-connoting architectural archetype from which every university building in the world is derived. I have had cause to visit several over the years, in different countries and on different continents, and whether they are out-of-town campuses or city-centre institutions, revered seats

of learning touting their medieval origins or brash new setups
proud of their sleek postmodernism, whether redbrick, neoclassical, brutalist or Gothic, they are all instantly and utterly
recognisable as being universities.

The one I found myself in at that very moment, for example,
had a fine if somewhat grubby neoclassical facade as its opening statement, graced by a long sweeping staircase for students
to slump on, smoke and sleep, leading to a huge doorway that
fed into a gloomy atrium lined by busts of the place's found-
ing fathers. Corridors sneaked off in every direction, each one
a door-lined strip-lit tunnel, tatty felt noticeboards flecked with
thumbtacked class lists, exam results, seminar times, announce-
ments of the adjacent officeholders' latest dreary publications,
invitations to experimental drama groups, hints of desperation
ever seeping through their poorly set type. Always, the university has brief flurries of intense activity followed by hours or
even weeks of dusty silence and echoing emptiness, the weeks
where academics shuffle around the corridors to be caught only
out of the corner of your eye, should you be looking.

I had been in that lecture theatre many times before: long low
benches, chipped white walls, a computer ever awaiting an absent
technician to bring it to life, a sliding chalkboard, harsh lights.

I apologise for the digressions. Such abstract thoughts often
take me over in moments like these. I sat observing the harsh
lights as the Profesora spoke to me.

"A politic book," said the Profesora. "Always difficult." I
hadn't been invited to her office this time. She'd decided to give
me her opinion from the front row where she had sat for the best
part of the previous hour, scowling under a Kandinsky scarf.

"I like difficult," I said. "I _do_ difficult. I do not shy away from
difficult."

"This I like, but there is difficult, and there is difficult. This kind of difficult, hmmm."

"I'm afraid I don't follow, Profesora."

"In our country, our small country, too there was a book." She glanced at the Assistant. "*The Waltzing Tree*. Martin Hambach. Hambach had to go to Switzerland. He writes for television now." There was little regard in the way she said "television." "I think it is now available, but no one would want to read it. Not a good book. A group of peasants meet under a tree to go dancing. That's about it. But people started copying them, because the book was very success, very wide read. So these groups of people, meeting by night out in the country. The government then, they didn't like such activity."

"But surely things are different now."

"In our small country, things are always different, and things are always the same." I made a mental note to put this line in my notebook as soon as possible, and also to trace its provenance. *The Leopard*, was it? I think that may have been at the heart of the Profesora's occasionally impressive oration: half-remembered quotations.

I muttered something about freedom of the imagination, unacknowledged legislators, the validity of fiction, but the Profesora seemed little disposed to engage in debate and more concerned by the fact that she had lost her cigarettes.

"Not everything is story, Doctor. Some things are true." I looked at the Assistant. The Assistant nodded. They were right after all. I was dismissed.

I SLUNK BACK TO the ? café where I had decided to become resident and slumped in my window seat, smoking one of the Profesora's cigarettes. Sleight of hand isn't a trick only narrators should know. I consoled myself by recognising that she hadn't been as grumpy as the previous week, and the students had done that banging on their desks thing again, although there had been noticeably fewer of them in attendance than the previous week. I hoped none of them would get into trouble as a result of their enthusiasm but had also noticed a few moments of deep, awkward silence as I spoke, the kind that descends when one has made an innocent yet deeply embarrassing faux pas. It is a fault of mine, the ability to be ridiculously oversensitive about some things while being brutally ignorant of others. Lamenting my own paucity of research, I dug my notebook from the pocket of my overcoat that I had draped over the seat next to me and began to write.

~

"WHAT ARE YOU writing?"

"That's not a question that one should ask."

"Why not?"

"It's intrusive. And it may be about you. What are you doing here, anyway?"

"Everyone comes here."

"I hope the Profesora doesn't."

"I've come to talk to you about her." I was worried the

Assistant had been sent to warn me of my impending arrest for theft of personal property and tried to move the offending cigarettes discreetly back into my pocket. Sensing that my discretion had not been discreet enough, I tried to change the subject.

"Have you found where Guyavitch's grave is?"

"Ah, yes, I think I know, though it is a long time since I have seen it," she replied, blithely ignoring my clumsy prestidigitation and attempts to derail her.

"Can we visit?"

"I hope so, yes. I will take you."

"Would the Profesora like to come too?"

"Ah, no. It is better not to talk of Guyavitch to her."

"Whyever not?"

"He is still a controversial writer in our country, I'm afraid."

"But he's so little known, how can he possibly be controversial?" I asked.

"Precisely because he is so little known." Before I could even attempt to untangle her logic, the Assistant continued.

"But I am here because she would like to invite you to dinner, the day after tomorrow." I remembered such an invitation already having been extended, but confess I had forgotten it over the last week, immersed as I had been in the planning of my lectures and wanderings through the city.

"Why did she send you to ask me?"

"Because I am her Assistant. I carry messages."

"I see. Well, tell her that I'd be charmed."

"She isn't as bad as you think."

"You don't know how badly I think."

"Remember not to mention Guyavitch."

"I promise. Are you coming too?"

"Oh no. I am only the Assistant." And with that, she left.

Two nights later I found the Profesora waiting for me in the lobby, slightly less geometric and somewhat more colourful in a Miró-influenced pattern.

"We go now."

Outside, Jan was waiting for us. As if in deference to the occasion and the Profesora, he'd put on a black jacket over his orange football shirt and adopted a far less talkative manner. He opened the door for the Profesora (not for me), got into the front seat and drove us away.

We went round in seeming circles for a while until we reached a place I thought I recognised.

"Is this Liberation Square?" I asked.

"No, Revolution Square," replied the Profesora.

"I'm afraid they look very similar to me."

"It is said, yes. The architects were brothers. But they hated each other, and ended up killing each other in a duel fought with set squares and compasses."

Jan pulled up outside a row of closed shops. A signless metal door stood between a pork butcher and a watch repairer. The Profesora opened it and led the way in through a narrow tunnel with a low ceiling that gave onto a small, heavily wallpapered room with fewer than a dozen tables, each one for two people only.

"A place for talking," she said, then fell completely silent.

As I have already had cause to note, neither small talk nor polite conversation in general lie among my strengths. I am a man often happier in his own company. I find the practice of filling silence with speech for the sake only of filling that silence pointless. And yet the silence the Profesora maintained became deeply uncomfortable, mainly because the longer she remained silent the more I found myself wanting to do the one thing I had expressly been warned not to.

When a waiter eventually appeared and bid us good evening in perfect English, I wanted to reply, *Guyavitch*. The Profesora ordered directly, without consulting me or a menu, and when the waiter offered me a taste of wine I had to twist my tongue in order to say "good" and not *Guyavitch*. I thought about mentioning the weather, but the only adjective to describe it that came to mind was *Guyavitch*. Guyavitch, I wanted to say. Guyavitch guyavitch guyavitch.

I was glad when the food began to arrive. A flock of waitstaff descended at once, and within less than a minute the small table was piled with plates of smoky vegetable mush, beans swimming in yellowish oil, roast garlic, rank-smelling cheese redolent of the farmyard and pieces of burnt dead animal. A vast tureen of soup took centre table. The Profesora ladled some into a bowl and shoved it before me.

"Eat," she said. "This is good food. Eat everything." The soup was bright green and tasted of grass. She didn't touch it. She didn't eat anything, in fact, contenting herself instead with a new packet of cigarettes that she would spend the remainder of the evening smoking her way through.

"I'd hoped the Professor would come." She looked black. "He sends his apologies."

"Shall I ever get to meet him?"

"He has some health problems. But I'm certain you will."

Silence again. *Guyavitch*, whispered the demon in my head. I ate as much as I could to stop the word from coming out, and the more I ate, the better it tasted. The mushrooms were bosky, the artichokes ligneous, the cheese decidedly caprine and the kidneys had a fine tang of faintly scented urine, and by the time I had polished off the best part of the bottle of austere red, I found myself positively enjoying it.

"We were lovers once," she said.

"You and the . . . ?"

"Professor, yes. But no longer."

"I'm sorry."

"I am not. My husband didn't approve."

"I suppose not."

I was pleased when the plates were suddenly dispatched by the reappearing flock and a large glass of brandy placed before me. Trying to avoid the word "Guyavitch," I asked the other question I had been wanting to.

"When might it be possible to visit the library?" Although I hadn't been able to find much online, I was certain that the university would have a well-stocked library, given the Professor's specific research interests and the department's specialisms, after all.

"Library is rather difficult at this moment. The Professor will need to issue a special permission."

"Then I hope his health recovers soon."

The Profesora didn't acknowledge my hope and made to offer me a cigarette instead, but then said, "Of course, you don't smoke, do you?" I told her I'd make an exception at this point, just to be companionable.

"Will I be much longer in the hotel?"

"Is it not satisfactory?"

"A little claustrophobic, if I may be honest."

"There are stories about the place."

"Such as?"

"I don't deal in tattle-tittle."

I smoked, concentrating on the cigarette to avoid the silence and prevent myself from saying *Guyavitch*. She leaned in conspiratorially.

"You must know, Doctor, that things are complex at the university right now. Many changes are happening."

"Ah," I said. "Always the way."

"What way?"

"I mean, universities. Always changing!"

"No, Doctor. This is not a mere question of administration."

"No?"

"No. You see, they are trying to kill me."

"Who, the university? The Professor?"

"All. All of them."

"I'm sorry."

"I am not. I shall win."

She ordered more coffee for herself, and I decided I needed another brandy.

~

JAN WAS STILL waiting outside when we'd done, and still not speaking. I think the jacket had quelled his odd loquacity, though he did catch my eye in the rearview mirror, as if he wanted to say something but could not. We sped back to the hotel in silence, and as we pulled up the Profesora spoke.

"Now you are of my part, you must help. Next lecture, Doctor, we expect."

"Guyavitch!" I coughed.

"What?"

"Nothing, sorry, a slight cough, that's all."

"Good night, Doctor. We expect of you. And remember: even if the sky was crooked, it wouldn't be any lower."

~

THE NEXT MORNING I sat in the ? café considering which book I would be remonstrated with for discussing next and watching the few other customers play the odd chess-like game which seemed so popular here. Like many of us, I suspect, I lead a strange alternative life, one parallel to my real one, in which I am not a perma-skint jobbing writer and critic, but instead have a simple, useful occupation. In this alternative life, for example, I may find myself running a café such as this one, passing the time serving coffee and wiping glasses, engaging regulars in pleasantries, untroubled by ambition or thwarted desire. I ignore the dull reality of grudging customers, greedy suppliers, tax returns, endless hours and business rates, and instead imagine myself a contented artisan. For there are, surely, contented souls out there somewhere, aren't there?

After a few fruitless hours writing, I went to pay the bill for the surprisingly large amount of coffee I seemed to have drunk, pulled a note from my wallet and handed it to the barman. He took it gingerly, rubbed it between his thumb and finger then held it up to the light.

"No," he said. "Not good," and handed it back. I looked at the note again, and it looked fine to me. I wondered what could be wrong with it. Seeing my bafflement he took another identical note from his till and held it out for comparison. "See," he said, pointing to the figure of the heavily moustached man who graced the grubby bluish note. Indeed, on the note I held, the man had no moustache. I was even more baffled, wondering how I could have been taken in by such a rudimentary forgery, and who could have passed it off to me. I thought about Jan the taxi but remembered he hadn't offered me any change at all. This had been the only other place where I'd spent any money. At this point the barman shrugged and said, "Ach, no problem," and accepted the first-offered note. "I give it to someone else. All the same."

I was to come across several of these notes over the next few weeks, and always checked to see if the man had a moustache or not. Sometimes he did, sometimes he didn't. Forgery, it seemed, was rife, and largely accepted.

Tales of literary forgery were rife in the world that I then inhabited,[3] and the incident set my mind to thinking of recounting one of them in my next lecture, but I could come up with little that was fresh or interesting. I did, however, have a book which had a wider story attached to it, and following a no-doubt-connected anxiety dream involving me drowning in a book-filled basement, black water rising slowly around me and a locked door, sodden pages floating past my eyes, I decided that it would be the right thing for the next lecture.

---

[3] The reader is directed to the story of Eric Quayne in the *BDLF*, entry no. 30.

The Dark Monarch by John Brisling

England is a strange country, if it is indeed a country at all. From Celtic Cornwall to Viking Northumbria, global London to the flatlands of the Eastern coast, from the "lost" county of Hookland to the strange, time-stopped town of Scarfolk, this small, rainy island anchored off the coast of Europe is often a mystery even to those who were born and grew up there.

Far from the sanctioned history of deference to crowns, tea-drinking and moderation in everything lies a different country, one anarchic and ever shifting, a shore for tides of settlers and migrants, stratified, complex, hidden. This England, England the lesser-known, is the country of straw bears and selkies, burry men, molly dancers, the Garland King and Jacks-in-the-green, of apotropaic magic, will-o'-the-wisps and standing stones, a land of troubled psychic geography, dislocated, belligerent, haunted. It is to this largely hidden tradition that our next book belongs. However, we are not going to look at some ancient grimoire, nor a treatise on witchcraft, nor some spurious Arthuriana, but something far more modest-seeming. John Brisling's *The Dark Monarch* was published as a cheap paperback by the children's imprint Puffin Books in 1962. The book has had a strange life, as we shall see.

It begins with two children, David and Mary, brother and sister, twins. No time is mentioned, but we assume that the story is taking place in their present, an England still slowly recovering from the war, grasping to find its new identity. They live in a small house on the edge of a council estate, a liminal place, halfway between the town and the country, neither one nor the other. While part of their identity is urban, they are drawn to the open land that is receding from the increasingly built up environment: we learn that a power station is being built within view of their house, pylons are beginning to stride across the open fields and low rolling hills, a vision of a glistening future, the white heat of technology. Yet decay too surrounds them—there are still bombed-out buildings and a disused Second World War airstrip plays a prominent role.

Their father has disappeared, they live with their mother, a woman who is herself curiously absent, spending much time sitting alone on the sofa, staring into space, living on nothing but bread and butter and drinking weak tea. Today's reader recognises her as suffering from some sort of depression, but this knowledge is not accessible to David and Mary, who only think their mother either ill or sad, and relish the freedom her isolation lends them.

It's a good, solid start for a young person's fantasy novel: a reality, perhaps not one too dissimilar to that of the intended readership, is quickly established. We know where we are, and yet there are undercurrents, hints that all is not quite idyllic. The prose is simple, almost as flat as the land which surrounds the characters. Good storytelling often does not need flashy pyrotechnics, a simple statement of facts is enough. Soon, though, we find ourselves having to question what those facts are.

David and Mary escape from their dull home life by running off to find adventures in the land around them. David imagines himself an airman, taking off or returning to the airstrip, while Mary is a heroic resistance fighter, capturing German spies. They go out at night, have camping expeditions, taking their own sandwiches and stolen bottles of pop, fashioning a makeshift tent from old overcoats and sleeping in abandoned buildings or under the stars. David is in love with the possibilities of the future he sees developing around him, while Mary mourns the passing of the countryside she so loves.

One place, in particular, fascinates them: Black Mirror Pond, an expanse of water which may have once serviced a nearby mill (now abandoned, of course). The name is apposite: the pond is particular in the unforgiving stillness and utter opacity of its surface. They try to fish there but catch nothing. They think of swimming, but the water is always too cold and forbidding, even for their toes. And yet, they are always drawn there.

One day, returning from Black Mirror Pond, they hear an argument going on inside their house. Eavesdropping, they hear a man they don't know, angry with their mother, constantly talking about a boy, "Colin," and blaming her for his death. They go in and the man slinks away, hardly looking at them. At first their mother is dismissive about the incident, but eventually tells them they once had an elder sibling, a boy, six years older than them who had died when they were but babies. *Drowned, he did, in Black Mirror Pond.*

It's a stark note in what until this point had been an almost idyllic, escapist fantasy, and not the turn the reader had perhaps been expecting.

The story continues, the reason for their mother's depression revealed, and David and Mary become ever more attracted to the old pond. David hatches the strange idea that his elder brother still lives, that he has merely passed through the "Black Mirror" and is alive, in some form, on the other side of it. He grows more and more convinced of his idea, eventually managing to convince his more sceptical sister as well. They dare each other to go in.

This is a portal fantasy in some ways, but there is no magic wardrobe or secret garden here, just murky black water, familiar to anyone who grew up on the edge of a British town.

Told that their mother is too sick to look after them, the children are then sent away to the home of a distant aunt. This takes up the second part of the book. Brisling describes in some detail the long train journey that takes them there, the provincial railway stations where they change and wait before eventually arriving in deep countryside, this time far from any civilisation. *A house that looked like it had been quarried from the hills itself, rough-hewn boulders held together with moss and lichen.* The aunt is elderly and deeply eccentric yet seems benevolent. Like Mary, she is one for the countryside, and never shops but brews up evil-smelling soups from nettles, weeds and hedgerow berries. She makes them drink tea made from dried wildflowers. The children are again lost, but ever resourceful they begin to make themselves a new home in this strange place. They rapidly forget not only their initial homesickness, but their home itself, and their mother. Another idyll is briefly established, until there is a visitor. The angry, bitter man who had argued with their mother shows up at the aunt's house, letting himself in, helping himself to food, speaking to no one. *Who is he?* the children ask. He's your father, replies the aunt.

The third and final section of the book returns them to their home, but a home that is now very different to them. Things begin to get increasingly strange. The book, which has up until now been notable for its clarity, precision and simplicity, morphs into something very different, a territory of vision and hallucination as realist moorings are slipped, the past returns, engulfing the present and dragging the future into it. The mirror shatters, and unleashes—what? Even having read the book several times, it is difficult to say. We know that the figure of the "Dark Monarch" is loosed, without ever being sure quite who or what he is. Time stretches and shifts back on itself as the children become adults then children again, apparently fighting a battle against forces they barely comprehend, in several different epochs. Some contemporary reviewers tried to liken it to both *The Lord of the Flies* and *The Lord of the Rings*, but the comparison is weak. What it actually resembles, or prefigures, is something more like the oneiric opacity of the ending of Kubrick's *2001*, or a Nicolas Roeg film, had Roeg chosen the English hinterland rather than the Australian outback to baffle and confound.

Without giving too much away, the book ends with a balance achieved, a strange kind of harmony, a restoration. The book has shown not only what is strange in the familiar, but also what is familiar in the strange. But, as David and Mary find, nothing can ever be restored in the form that you want it. Everything will return, but it will return altered, so much so that you won't recognise it even when it comes. Sometimes we don't recognise such things until it is too late.

It's worth considering how much of the book reflects John Brisling's own experiences. Born in London in 1933, he was an evacuee during the war, put on a train by his mother, sent away to a small town in the Welsh Marches. For the next two years the only thing he heard from his family was that his father had gone missing in action, presumed dead somewhere in the western desert.

In his memoir, *Lost Hours and Days*,[4] he vividly describes his overwhelming memory of the time. Doing some work on the kitchen of the farmhouse where he was staying, workmen found a bellarmine or "witch bottle" buried under the threshold. With scant regard for either antiquity or superstition, they broke it open to find a mummified cat inside. The practice was not uncommon throughout much of Britain, he discovered, possibly as an attempt to ward off evil, but equally likely to be a curse placed on someone, or some place. When he eventually returned to London, he found

---

[4] Thomson & Thompson, 1968.

that his mother had been killed too, by a stray firebomb during the Blitz. He spent the next few years living with his aunt, until he left for university (a scholarship to Cambridge, which he hated), and never returned to the capital.

The Dark Monarch was his third book and (apart from his memoir) the last thing he wrote. The first two books, *The Midsummer Ghost* and *The House in the Fog*, hinted at what he was capable of, but are adequate at best, neither particularly interesting. They are still, however, regularly found in charity shops in the U.K. for but a few pennies. This, let me point out, is not the case with *The Dark Monarch*. I have only once found a copy, but a tattered paperback, in an antiquarian bookshop in Wales. The bookseller wanted £500 for it, a sum which, were I a wealthier man, I would have parted with.

So why has this strange situation arisen? There are, I believe, several reasons for this. The first one may be obvious—although Brisling only hints at it in his memoir, his publishers were not at all happy about this turn toward a darker and more complex style, that third section in particular. Stubbornly, Brisling refused to change a word, which, in turn, led the publishers to print but a very small run of the book and give it almost no publicity whatsoever, feeling that it would fail before it had begun, realising it was the last work in Brisling's three-book contract. In the few places it was reviewed, the book was described only briefly and unfavourably, found lacking in comparison to its peers. Critics picked up on obvious things: the children never go to school, they are too knowing for their age, the plot draws on too many stock tropes and so on and so on. Few copies in the already small print run sold.

It's hardly surprising. Books about England were highly unfashionable for a time, as if somehow intrinsically jingoistic or just plain dull. There was an element of the cultural cringe in many critics' attitudes, not wanting to recognise this old mud-smelling stuff in favour of American glamour or European chic. The book was badly mismarketed: it should perhaps have been shelved closer to Robert Aickman than Alan Garner, and as an early example of the folk horror genre, a predecessor of David Rudkin and Alan Clarke's television film *Penda's Fen* perhaps, it went unrecognised.

That said, however, I think one of its problems is that although it may bear superficial similarities to other works, it is in fact quite unlike any other work of fiction I know. As well as folk horror, the book can also be seen as an early piece of nature writing, a genre then largely unrecognised. Mary's sections of the book involve meticulous, precise descriptions not only of the flora and fauna, but also of the deeper lie of the land, the result of careful watching and thinking. It came out the same year as Rachel Carson's *Silent Spring* to which it is curiously analogous with its sense of threat, of a world in imbalance. And while the land has power, has agency, its relationship with humanity is never discounted—they know that people have made the land, as much as the land has made the people. This is writing about nature which does not discount its often brutal history: one of enclosure, land grabs, dispossession and disenfranchisement, the industrial revolution and the technological one coming. And yet the nature revealed in *The Dark Monarch* is nature that couldn't care less about where people draw their boundaries onto it. This is the land, chthonic, ancient, as undisturbed by man as by a fly.

It's also worth noting that the original title of the book was "The Drowned Man," which I take not only to be a reference to a non-canonical tarot card, but also an oblique nod to T. S. Eliot. The drowned man would be the missing brother, but also bears the same initials as the Dark Monarch himself, a possible key to reading the book, and a possible explanation as to the identity of this mysterious character.

Names are slippery in the book, but naming is a kind of magic itself. Naming things means having power over them. If we change the names for things, then we alter that power. But what are the true names of things? How do we know really?

The prog-folk band Comus were said to be working on a concept LP based on the book, but none of the recordings have ever surfaced. Meanwhile, certain secondhand book grubbers have dedicated their lives to the pursuit of the book, scouring the country whenever the slightest rumour goes out that one has been spotted in whatever condition.

This is an indication however, that the book is not forgotten, and is finally beginning to be re-remembered. A Kickstarter campaign has been set up to fund a film of it, but sadly not enough backers have yet been found who can agree on the project. The book is so enigmatic and elusive that each person who has been lucky enough to read it seems to have a completely different understanding of it. It is the destiny of such works to disappear and then be rediscovered, as if they too were artefacts that had gone under the soil for many years. Perhaps it is our greater awareness of the delicate balance in which we live with our home planet.

I wonder though if the reason isn't simpler: Is it simply because the book is so damn disturbing? Has it cast a talismanic power? Has it brought about its own disappearance, its own slip into a half-world of folk memory?

Mostly, however, I suspect the reason the book is so rare is simply because in 1965, Brisling himself bought up every copy of it he could find and destroyed all of them (again according to his memoir). He gives no reason for his actions, other than saying that he was disappointed with its reception and didn't want the albatross of a failed novel around his neck. Nobody knows what happened to him after that. The jacket note on *Lost Hours and Days* stated only that "John Brisling is a writer who lives in England." Even his publishers didn't know his address, it was said, though there were rumours: he'd become a recluse living in a bothy on the North Yorkshire Moors, he'd moved to Wales and started hand-carving wooden furniture, he'd joined a cult and gone to Findhorn, he'd gone mad. None of these were true it turned out.

~

There is a coda to this story, if I may. I once met John Brisling, or at least I think I did. It took some time to track him down, as you may imagine, but by rifling through some old phone books, knocking on a few wrong doors, following up on a few leads and bits of gossip, I found him. He wasn't on a remote Scottish isle, nor had he joined the Hare Krishnas. He was living in a tiny house, not much more than a shed, in a remote village by the sea in Norfolk. I knocked on the door, a man who looked younger than I expected answered. He had long brown hair, thinning and greying slightly, and a bushy beard, but sufficiently resembled the photographs I'd seen of him some fifty years earlier not to make me doubt my step. I asked him if he was John Brisling. "Who wants to know?" he asked. I told him I was a literary scholar who was interested in his work. "No, I'm not," he replied. Nevertheless, he invited me in and made tea in a huge brown teapot. Every inch of the small, damp, sea-rotten house was covered with bookshelves. I sat on a broken chair and scanned the spines, half-hoping to see dozens of copies of *The Dark Monarch*, but there were none. They were mostly broken-backed airport thrillers and '70s soft porn. He brought the tea through, poured it into a dirty mug with a broken handle. An empty sardine can sat on the table, making do as an ashtray. He rolled a joint, smoked the whole thing himself and said absolutely nothing. When I'd finished my tea I asked him again if he was John Brisling. He shook his head. I thanked him for his time, then got up and left. I'd seen enough, and knew I wasn't going to get anything out of him. As I walked off I turned round, just for a second, and he was standing in the doorway, watching me, making sure I was leaving, muttering something under his breath.

I cannot say why, but as I walked off, I found myself certain that the man was in fact Brisling, and I wondered what he'd done to himself, what strange power he had unleashed with that one book. It is always dangerous. By writing about something, you make it real.

Thank you.

I FELT SLIGHTLY NERVOUS as the lecture finished because—although the response had been appreciative—I was aware I hadn't told the whole truth. Sometimes there is too much for a lecture to hold.

While the story about finding and meeting the man who may or may not have been Brisling (even though I'd assured the audience he was, I myself have never really been sure) was all true, there had been more—the problem being that much of it was simply too barmy to countenance stuffing into what I felt was already a dangerously over-packed lecture.

In truth, once Brisling had smoked his spliff and finished off the entire pot of tea, he had started talking. "All living things are holy," he'd begun, "that's what they say. And they're right, but it's not enough—not only *living* things—*everything* is holy. All matter is holy. The Gawain poet knew this. Blake knew this. And amongst matter, *books* are the holiest of all. What is the most primal form of matter? Yes, that's right—the tree! And books come from trees, of course, primal matter forged into knowledge, truth, lies, wishes, dreams, curses, plots—everything! All of everything. And that is why books are so holy. Destroying a book is tantamount to murder, *worse* than murder. That is why I keep them all. I must save them, all of them." He waved his hands over the boxes and boxes of biblious crap he had piled around him, then fixed me with his bloodshot eyes. "The water is coming, I know, and the water will take us back. But the water too, is holy."

I have heard a lot of stoner bullshit in my time, I have occasionally engaged in it, possibly even produced some of it myself, but this was something else. To be clear, I liked his idea in principle, yet the manner of its delivery was disturbing to say the least. I bid my leave and gently got up to go, but as I was going he asked me a question.

"You want to know who the Dark Monarch is?" He laughed and pointed to the mangy books ranked around him. "These, these are the Dark Monarchs. Books are the Dark Monarchs. Now fuck off and never come back."

~

THE MEMORY OF this unpleasant, though undeniably fascinating, encounter made me feel much better about my post-lecture meeting with the Profesora, today seated in her office resplendent in a Sonia Delaunay—inspired dress/scarf combo that gave her a disconcertingly approachable appearance. My positive impressions were soon dispelled.

"A children book? This is the Department of Literature, Doctor."

"Some works originally intended for children are some of the finest works of literature we have, Profesora." I had decided to stand my ground.

"And you believe this one of them?"

"What makes 'greatness,' Profesora?"

"Not my farmyard. Yours."

I wanted to tell her how I believed that literary greatness wasn't an innate quality but something formed through the machinations of culture and society and history. I wanted to talk about the subtle formation of canons and discriminations against particular kinds of taste and style, about race and gender and nation, but it would have to wait for another lecture, perhaps, as she had already moved on.

"And a politic book, too. We agreed on no politic books."

I wanted to say how all books are, essentially, political, given that they form part of the cultural fabric, that they play a role in the national imagination, that all stories have consciences, but to no avail.

"Children politic books the worst, I think. *Little Peter's Hands.* Banned here during the Times. You know it, I think?" I confessed that I didn't, and assured her I would seek it out. "Don't bother. Not a great book. I go now. Make the pig squeal next week, Doctor!" She waved her hand dismissively, and I was gone.

I MUST SAY THE Profesora's critique smarted particularly badly that week, precisely because of her assertion that I was dealing with mere children's literature. For many of us, books are our childhood friends and formative experiences. It was an early encounter with a book which, I suspect, had led me to where I found myself right at that moment.

The problem is, I cannot remember *which* book.

As a just-literate child, I had once come across a book in our local library that possessed me. I remember little to nothing of its plot, none of its characters and scarcely any of its words, let alone its title or author, yet that book has haunted me ever since. I remember it as filled with smoke and fire, shadow and flame. I remember its utter mystery and infinite possibility. I was lost, captivated.

The book, of course, had to be returned to the library, and each week I went back there, hoping to borrow it again. I never did. I picked out book after book after book and scoured their pages and pictures and jackets, trying to find a turn of phrase or an illustration I recognised, something which brought the story back to me, but even though I sometimes came close, I never found it again.

I have been looking for that book ever since.

This, I know, is what has led me to plough this furrow, what set me out on this life of rummaging through the rubbish bins of literature, of being forever targeted by shady book dealers or led on wild chases for scarcely known writers, of vainly trying to re-create the sensation of that book using my own poor words. I am trying to find something I cannot ever be sure actually existed, something I myself may have imagined.

CURIOSITY SUFFICIENTLY AROUSED, I tried to find out more about *Little Peter's Hands* later that day, as the Assistant and I were walking around hopelessly lost in an attempt to find Guyavitch's grave. She'd been waiting outside the Profesora's office as I was dismissed, as if ready to take me.

"A cruel tale," she said of the book as we hit yet another dead end. "A little boy gets separated from his hands."

"Separated?"

"Yes. His hands go missing, and he has to find them."

"And why was it banned?"

"The Overcoat thought it was about him."

"The who?"

"The Overcoat. The Moustache. The Spectacles. There were many names for him."

"I see. And was the book about him?"

"The Overcoat thought everything was about him."

"Was it?"

"Mostly, yes."

~

I'VE MENTIONED THE city's labyrinthine qualities already, and do not wish to bore the reader with endless descriptions of streets either residential or commercial, but I must point out how the streets both were and weren't replicas of one another.

Aside from the duelling brothers who had fought over the apparently identical Liberation and Revolution Squares, other parts of the city had been laid out on a grid system, but the story was that the architects and engineers responsible for their construction had used faulty equipment (or so the Assistant told me), so two streets which should have run parallel did not, regular corners became acute or obtuse angles, the system of numbering buildings went completely awry—it was just as possible that a number 163 would be followed by a 27 as by a 164.

Added to this there was the Old Town, which was not one central area, as in many cities, but a dispersive arrangement of small collections of late medieval and early modern buildings which appeared in small pockets all over the place. What I had assumed to be a river turned out to be two rivers, both of which wound their way through the city in a haphazard fashion, having been channeled and twisted by the hand of man as much as that of nature. Even those native-born to the city got lost here. It was a city designed to lose oneself in.

And so we had. I'd walked with the Assistant for more than an hour in search of Guyavitch's grave, and it was as elusive to us now as it had ever been. The Assistant seemed certain that it was in a small graveyard, a tiny unkempt patch of land between two tall buildings, guarded only by a rusting iron railing and some long grass. That, at least, was how it was in her memory, but memory makes up its own stories every time.

"I visited over twenty years ago," she said, making me wonder how old she might be. "I used to walk off on my own, and one day I came across the place by chance."

Several promising spaces appeared, but none revealed much more than a few empty bottles, discarded clothes and burned-out mattresses, let alone anything resembling a tombstone.

Our wandering was not fruitless, however, for it was during our search that I came across the first of the city's two second-hand bookshops.

As I suspect many readers of this book already know, bookshops are a strange kind of utopia. Whether a bright, shining emporium, perhaps a link in an international chain, with a sleek interior featuring gleaming lights bouncing off miles of polished wood shelves and white surfaces, tables heaving under the joyous multiplicity of their piled wares, an embedded café and a list of forthcoming reader events, a handsome uniformed staff eager to help; or the random independent housed in an odd building, all stairs and tiny rooms with a unique stock of haphazardly ordered single copies, a lone curmudgeon seated behind a desk stacked with uncollected orders and unpaid bills; or the second-hand bookshop, possibly feigning an attempt at antiquarianism, enveloped in that damp lignin smell and particular quality of silence as the books absorb the sound of footsteps but amplify the rustle of their pages, the consequent wondering about the provenance and history of the stock, the fascination of the detritus of other people's lives, the overripe plenitude of the laden shelves, an absent owner (if there is a cat so much the better). Brisling's curious statement about the holiness of books begins to resonate when thus considered.

That day's discovery, however, was none of these. It was squashed between two tall buildings, a covered alleyway leading to the ever-mysterious back room (and what bookshop does not possess one?), its walls lined with heaving shelves leading to a dim and distant ceiling. No ladder was available to aid with consulting the upper shelves, but the shorter of stature were catered to with a number of heavily piled tables just below knee height. At eye level, the books were kept in locked cupboards, their spines visible through chicken wire doors.

"You have to call the owner should you wish to view," whispered the Assistant, "but he is not a nice man."

Some of the books on the tables were shrink-wrapped, which led me to imagine something intriguingly filthy, but they turned out to be nothing more than standard paperback editions of world classics, marked up with an unfairly high price.

"New stock," called an unseen voice from the back room. The Assistant tugged at my sleeve encouraging us to leave, but it was too late. The voice had emerged, belonging to a man around whom I guessed the shop had been designed: six and a half feet tall, arms down to his knees. He glowered at us. Browsers were not welcome, it seemed.

"There are two bookshops in the city," the Assistant told me as we scuttled away. "The other one is run by his ex-wife. They hate each other. There are stories. They send thieves into each other's shops, they think everyone who enters is spying on the other. It is difficult to find good books in this city."

"It can be difficult to find good books in any city," I replied. "Good books are rare things."

"True," sighed the Assistant. "It is a shame about the library."

"What has happened to the library?"

"Didn't the Profesora tell you? The library has been dispersed."

"Dispersed?"

"Rehoused. Temporary, perhaps. Or perhaps not. For its own safety."

"She told me the Professor could give me a reader's card."

"She has a complex relationship with the truth, sometimes." She smiled again, and as she did so, I noted how her eyes almost, but not quite, disappeared.

I was glad that I had at least managed to spot a nice copy of Gilbert Pump's *Mr Eye* in the shop, and comforted myself by running my fingers over it, deep in the pocket of my overcoat. It more than made up for not being able to find Guyavitch's resting place, an adventure which would have to wait for another occasion, because now it was late, and getting dark. There was a book to read, a barstool and a glass waiting for me, as well as another lecture to fret about, and an anxiety dream to have.

T HE DREAM KINDLY held off for the next week, until the night before my fourth lecture, and when it came it was almost depressingly banal: not being able to find the lecture theatre, climbing up an endless narrow stairwell and knocking on countless unresponsive doors. My subconscious was letting me down there; it could do better.

Especially given that, when the morning came, I found the lecture theatre without difficulty and merely a fashionable five minutes late. (I'd made the mistake of waiting for Jan to show. He didn't.) As I walked into the lecture theatre, the Profesora and the Assistant were already installed on the front row. The Profesora beckoned me to her and leaned forward conspiratorially.

"Doctor, there is news. We have an apartment for you. You will leave the hotel this evening."

"Excellent."

"And more news. The Professor is in the audience today. He is excitable to hear your lecture."

I tried not to let this make me nervous as I began.

Farewell Sweet Prince by Kurt Blankenberg

I know you're listening, it begins.

> *I know you can hear me. My voice is in these words and even though I am far away now, I know you are reading this. All well and good. Listen to me; I have things to tell you.*

It then shifts, this portentous opening, to a more sober style of narration, one which might be more expected in a crime novel (for such this is) as the narrator begins to tell his story.

> *It was late evening, sometime in October. I remember the light fading and the dark thickening in the streets of this city we love so well. I'd been to the Guapo's for a drink, stopped off at the Blind Cat after that where I ran into Lucien and the Crip—you remember them, don't you? You never liked them, I know, and—as it turned out—perhaps you were right not to. I was wearing my best suit—I call it "my best suit," though to be honest it was the only one I had. Times were tough back then, though they'd get tougher.*

~

The idiom speaks to us clearly nearly a century later (beautifully translated here from Blankenberg's original French by a sadly anonymous translator—the only copy in English I have been able to trace, and from which I now quote, is now held in Scotland Yard's Black Museum). It may lack the wit and spark of Chandler or the toughness of Spillane, but we're in that universe—or at least we seem to be, though there is much more to it than that. *Farewell Sweet Prince* predates those masters of crime writing by more than two decades and though it is roughly contemporary with early Christie, Blankenberg is drawing from a very different well. There is so much more to this book, as you will find out if you stay with me. I, too, have a story to tell you.

Let's step back a little. The story is known: If it didn't exactly begin then, crime fiction first flourished in the late nineteenth century. Fearful of the restless mobilising proletariat, crime fiction provided a narrative template in which the prevailing bourgeois order was temporarily broken, only then for it to be reaffirmed with the eventual apprehension of the criminal element. This leads to the view that crime writing is a fundamentally conservative genre—an idea which persists, not least in the reappearance of a strange genre known as "cosy crime," the perplexing oxymoron usually involving a country house, a profligate aristocrat and/or dodgy understairs staff, the plot a locked box or fiendish clockwork mechanism, a puzzle to be solved much as if it were a particularly tricky cryptic crossword. The view that crime writing is somehow reactionary or even escapist is one that has been much challenged by many later writers and critics who have justly pointed out that there is little that is "cosy" about murder of any kind, and instead point to the genre's preoccupation not only with greater questions of crime, punishment and morality but also note the way it deals with issues such as police corruption or social decay, and how it often includes unflinching descriptions of life at the fringes and margins of the contemporary world. This latter form would later be named with the catch-all terminology of "pulp."

While there are no country houses or homicidal butlers in

Farewell Sweet Prince, we do have a limited cast of characters, each one with his or her own secrets, a very tangible setting (of which more later) and a narrator whom we may not always trust. Similarly, while there are no wisecracking, .38-toting, trilby-wearing tough guys, there is booze, and lots of it, there is gambling and there is, inevitably, a femme fatale. But this is a work which is neither cosy nor pulp.

To return to the text:

It was late when I left them, I can't remember where exactly. We'd stopped off for a few more, then they said they were heading off to Deza's for a game.

"Come on!" They enticed me, jeered me, but I knew they only wanted my money. The thing they didn't know was that I no longer had any to lose.

I wasn't really staying anywhere at the time, you remember how rootless I was, so was thinking of where I could go to find a place to sleep for the night. As it got later I almost regretted not having gone with them to Deza's. At least I could have laid my head on his couch, woken there in the morning sometime, stolen some coffee and whatever was still lying around on the table before slipping off again. I think I'd vaguely thought of heading to Portuguese Rosa's for the night—go on, don't be jealous, that would be so stupid now—so that was the reason why I'd gone down to the river. Yes, I wish I'd gone to Deza's with Lucien and the Crip, that would have been better for everybody, as it turned out.

I was kicking along the towpath, black as pitch at that time, even the few lights that sometimes cast down onto the water were out by then, but it was still warm I remember, given the time of year. It was then that I saw something floating in the water, just a bundle of old rags or papers I thought at first. The gentle flow of the river was eddying it, the thing lightly riding the river's slow tide until it snagged on a branch and bumped off the stone bank. I still don't know why, I would have done best to leave it, whatever it was, but my curiosity was piqued—and you remember, don't you, how I always had that terrible curiosity, that need to know everything about everything, it'd be the death of me you once said. How right you were.

As soon as I bent down to take a closer look, I knew it was a body. A dog I thought at first, an old one maybe someone couldn't take care of anymore and had slung in the river. There were country people still around there then, that's how they treated their animals, no sentimentality. I felt shame for them, sad for the animal (even though I already knew it was far too big to be a dog) and hauled it—with some difficulty—up onto the riverbank. You know, of course, don't you? You know now, but still, let me tell you. Of course I realised it was a body, and a woman at that. Before I'd even got her out the sodden mass of old paper she'd been wrapped in fell away and I saw a leg with a tattoo at its ankle.

It was too late.

The thin, bony and slightly tumefied head wore a grimace. It was inclined to one side, with the black hair sticking to the temples, and the lids raised, displaying the dull globes of her eyes. The twisted lips were drawn to a corner of the mouth in an atrocious grin, and a piece of blackish tongue appeared between the white

teeth. It wasn't the first dead body I'd seen, and it wouldn't be
the last, but it was the worst—and of course, you know why, don't
you? Yes, it was you that I had dragged out of the river.

"Announcing a truth involves the stipulation of an enigma," wrote
Roland Barthes and even though he was describing a Poe story, his
words apply perfectly here. We find out who the body is, and it is not
who we expect. Aside from its narrative panache, though, it may be
worth wondering at this point about a certain stock trope of crime
fiction: the brutally murdered woman as an incipit. I find this distasteful, to say the least, but there again, there is much about this
book that is distasteful. It goes on.

I can't describe the horror, I have no words, so I won't, because of
course, as I ran my sorrowful fingers across your lifeless, swollen
face I eventually reached a deep scar on the lower jaw. It wasn't
you after all, was it? It was your twin sister.

And one of our enigmas is solved. It turns out that Lorena, the
addressee's sister, had not of course merely drowned but had also
been brutally stabbed, and blood from her ends up on the narrator's
clothes, in his hair, on his hands—both literally and figuratively, as
it becomes clear that he had motive and opportunity. He is duly
arrested for the murder, claims innocence, is not believed, manages
to escape and so the story goes on, running and racing with doubles
and likenesses and mistaken signs as he tries to find the real culprit,
and he becomes both hunter and hunted—and haunted, as he cannot forget what he has seen, and what he turns out to have done.

Blankenberg is the master of the slow reveal. Bit by bit we learn
more of the unnamed narrator, who turns out to fill the trifecta of
roles required by the genre: He is an ex-detective who has become

a shady private investigator who in turn stumbles into a crime, the circumstances of which he is not unacquainted with. He has what we would today certainly recognise as a drink problem (one of the other stock tropes of the detective), but it goes unremarked upon here, as though heavy drinking and chain smoking were merely the standard behaviour of men at that time (which perhaps they were). He certainly has a complex interior life, as the reader will find out.

So, while this is a book which sets down its coordinates clearly—the gun is on the wall and is certainly used by act three—I am trying to argue that there is more to it than it may initially seem. While the noirish ambience anticipates Chandler, and the clockwork precision of the plot and occasionally clunking prose suggest Christie or Simenon, much of it draws on a source that would have been familiar to Blankenberg: late-nineteenth-century penny dreadfuls and the Fantômas books, above all. Moreover, it has been suggested that much crime fiction drew on the *fait divers* sections of the increasingly widespread cheap newspapers in France at that time, lurid descriptions of thefts and murders illustrated with early photographs or graphically imagined pencil sketches aimed at titillation more than information. (And a notable thing about this book, it has an incredible attention to texts: texts, corrupt or otherwise, run through it—notes, bills, letters, newspapers—and it is one such text that eventually causes the denouement.)

As we have noted, this is a story about a man with a complex interior life engaged with questions of action and inaction, of crime and its rewards and punishments, of the fate of an individual pitted against larger, darker forces. As such, it cannot but bring to mind Dostoevsky, Kafka, Zola. It has an Expressionist quality that makes us mindful of nothing so much as the wordless novels of Frans Masereel or Andrzej Klimowski, Blankenberg's words having the same effect as their stark lino- and woodcuts. Indeed—in one particularly disturbing scene—words themselves are cuts on the skin. Another writer (who I am sure must have read *Farewell Sweet Prince*, though I admit I can find no tangible proof of this fact) is Graham Greene, who would have disingenuously called it an "entertainment." This is the story of a man who certainly recognises "good" and "evil" as categories more imperative than mere "right" and "wrong," yet one who seems perfectly happy to blur the boundaries between the two.

In this way, it is a fantastically modern book, as it is also in its descriptions of the city in which the action plays out. The reader, perhaps with ingrained Paris-centrism, may envision the city as the French capital, but there is no reason for it to be so: the Eiffel Tower certainly does not appear in this book, nor a Seine bridge or a sleazy Pigalle bar.

One of the wonders of the book is that even though the story is not set in any specific city every reader (at least, the few with whom I have been able to converse) is convinced they know exactly which city it is set in. One says that, clearly, the reference to a certain street shows it is Marseille. No, says another, it's Prague, look at the description of the police building in chapter 5. Others insist that it is Berlin, London, Barcelona. This is a book which has utmost specificity, yet also a placelessness. We could be anywhere. We are in a city we know intimately (along with its protagonist) but at the same time one which is, or has become, utterly unrecognisable—as, too, is its protagonist.

This may reflect Blankenberg's own experience. The author, born in Poland, raised in Belgium, was a triple émigré and ended up in France almost by mistake. He himself was on the run, wanted in three countries for crimes ranging from extortion to forgery to debt, and took to the pen in order to make money (and how wonderful, despite the murky motivation, to imagine a day when such a thing was still possible, plausible—imaginable, even). Though there is never any mention of violent crime in his CV, the vivid descriptions in *Farewell* can easily lead us to believe that this was not a man unacquainted with it.

The book first appeared in France in the early 1920s,[5] though it seems to have almost immediately been pirated, and several corrupt texts were in circulation. To our question: Why did this powerful, disturbing work then vanish?

There are the usual reasons: many copies have simply disintegrated, the result of low-quality paper and time doing its work. Blankenberg's own disappearance, some years after the book's publication, cannot have helped. And yet there is more. The few original copies that have survived are now (as far as I know) all in the reserve section of the Bibliothèque nationale de France, and viewing is only permitted with authorisation from a university or a pass from the chief of the gendarmerie. Yes, we may hypothesize that this book has vanished because of a darker purpose.

In 1925, six months after the book's publication, a body wrapped in newspaper was dragged from the banks of the Seine. It was never identified, and no one was ever charged, but the similarity between this discovery and the events of the book did not go unnoticed. A year later, a certain Abel Surman killed his landlady (and, it was suggested in court, ex-lover) in a gruesome manner which we shall not recount, but which was identical to one of the most shocking passages in the book. In 1927, Joop Herjit was convicted of the killing of two women, one having been choked with the pages of a book, the other having words from that book carved on her body.

---

[5] The earliest known edition was published by Dupond & Dupont in 1924.

The book? Yes, *Farewell Sweet Prince*. Similar things happened in Lyon, Marseille, even as far afield as London and Brussels. In each case, the book itself was found to be if not quite the culprit, then the instigator of the grim crimes.

Of course, this is nonsense, we think. Such scares are generational—from Victorian gothic shockers to 1950s horror comics to '80s video nasties to current worries about first-person shooters. But the panic engendered here wasn't about crime novels in general (so many so "cosy" after all), but about this particular book. It may well be nonsense, but the question is worth asking: How far *do* books contribute to actually causing events in the physical world—be they good or bad? We like to tell ourselves that great literature builds empathy, provides insights into other worlds, ennobles the spirit and so on and so on—but if it can do that, then surely it also has the power to do the opposite.

This book, this frantic confession, a man justifying his life and its actions, is a deeply troubling work, a book which spills out of its confines. If any book had such power, the power to corrupt, to deform, to do the opposite of ennobling the spirit, it would be one like this.

I have indeed worried about quoting too much from this book, fearing that even a quotation may have some secondhand potency. If any of you, after listening to this, are tempted to carry out any acts of violence following this lecture, please don't, but please do let me know. It would be fascinating for my research.

The book ends with the resolution required by its genre but is also left deeply, unsettlingly open. While one enigma may be resolved, Blankenberg shows, other greater ones are set up. We are all part of a chain of actions over which we ultimately have so little agency. Our protagonist ends up redeemed, justified, yet also tainted. Innocent yet haunted. Free yet forever dragged back to what he has experienced, aware of his own complicity in evil. We are all complicit, he says. We have all committed crimes, however large or small, and we shall all face our retribution for them.

Thank you.

NEWLY REHOUSED, I sat at my impressive desk with its view over the river and lots of sky in the window reflecting on my day so far, taking a momentary break from finally unpacking the items I need to hand while working. I am a man of few possessions, but some travel with me everywhere. I'm far from obsessive, blessedly free from the need to have them arranged in any particular order, but as long as they're all there, I feel secure: a good knife, its blade always sharp and its purpose undefined; a Zippo cigarette lighter bearing its owner's initials (even though I have long given up serious smoking, there is something Promethean about the ability to create fire at a moment's notice); my copy of Guyavitch's *Nine Stories* (Petrovich & Golyadkin, 1938, dappled binding, deckled edges, rather foxed); a small plaster statue of San Gennaro, his head many times broken off and glued back on; a pile of notebooks, provenance unimportant, storehouses of my imperfect memory. They are not objects, these things, they are nouns, adjectives and transitive verbs ready to be rearranged into any story I want to tell.

The story I needed to tell now was that of the Professor, who had turned out to be a stuttering little man, smaller than the clothes he wore, eyes moving in every direction except mine. I'd been trying to pick him out while giving the lecture, but had incorrectly managed to identify only a broad-shouldered, tweed-jacketed greyhair who'd wandered in halfway through and turned out to be a lost philosopher instead. I'd never have noticed the Professor sitting there in his shabby little jacket, even though on speaking to him his Jean-Paul Sartre–meets–Peter Lorre demeanour did render him a striking specimen indeed.

It was the Profesora who introduced me to him, of course, towering over him as she gave her verdict (comparatively positive, though it did include the word "superficial"), and I couldn't help remembering what she had told me in the restaurant: the thought of the two as lovers forced its way into my mind and I had to force it out again very quickly. His eyes darted from left to right then right to left as he spoke.

"I haven't read the book, no. I prefer not to read. A few sentences of the prose is enough, I find, for me to feel the grain of it. I prefer to read *about*. The secondary literature is so much more fascinating, I find." It was an odd opinion, but one which on reflection I found myself having a certain amount of sympathy with. "But very well done, very well. I found the lecture . . . ," he struggled for the word, ". . . *variegated*," and even after he'd found it, neither of us seemed to be sure it was the right one.

I was content, however, and as I sat there carefully rearranging my things on the desk I felt I had, perhaps, finally found my swing with the lectures. Even though *Farewell Sweet Prince* was far from the best book I had talked about, and the story surrounding it was almost certainly pure hokum, I did have to entertain as well, as the Profesora had told me, and spinning a good crime yarn was always a sure way to do that.

"I trust you will be joining us later," said the Professor. "We have a most Eminent Writer visiting our city, for a public debate, and it shall be our honour to take her to dinner."

"Next week, I think the Eminent Writer is coming," corrected the Profesora, and then addressed me. "I am not sure if you will come or not." She told me the name of the Eminent Writer, and it was one I knew, and did not like. Nevertheless, I would have relished a dinner invitation, partly to escape the boredom of eating alone, and partly because I still wanted to talk to the Professor about the disappearing library and about Guyavitch, on the quiet, where the Profesora couldn't hear. A crowded dinner table might be the perfect place, though even as I thought that, I knew there was little that escaped her.

The apartment into which I had been moved and where I now sat arranging my desk turned out to be next door to the hotel. This odd coincidence had at least rendered my relocation seamless (the only hiccup being the bill—I had assumed the university would pay, but it seemed not. However, the concierge seemed content to send the bill to the mysterious German gentleman bearing my name who had not shown up to take the room), although Jan the Taxi appeared outside the hotel (wearing the orange football shirt again—I wondered if it was the same one, or if he had many that were similar) and duly put my cases in the boot of his car, drove about one metre, then ceremonially unloaded again.

I hadn't even had to pack my cases, as I had never unpacked. The two buildings were separated only by a small garden, which I had been unable to see from the hotel room owing to its curious incline and strange perspective.

Even though the two buildings stood adjacent, achieving the feat of being side by side while also backing onto each other (as I have pointed out, geometry is a loose concept in this city, a suggestion more than a law), they felt very different. I have a friend who is convinced that, in some particular way, buildings are living things, each embodying its own history, each having its own character, much like a person. I do not agree with him, but occasionally wonder if there is not some strange truth in his idea. Whereas the hotel was clearly a repressed middle-aged man harbouring a dark secret, the apartment building was a gracious woman of a certain age, long greying hair tied into a loose chignon, fine taste in wine and an intelligent wit.

The stairway I heaved my suitcases up was wide and welcoming, the third-floor landing spacious and airy with distant piano music drifting through it, the door to my new temporary home an impressive slab of varnished oak. A nameplate on the door had recently been unscrewed, leaving a darker space on the bright wood. The key slid gracefully into the door which, I was relieved to find, opened inward and gave onto a large, light room. I walked in, dropped my cases on the parquet floor and looked out of the window.

For a writer of any kind, a good view is essential. There are those who claim they prefer to be in a windowless space, or at least have their desks facing a wall. I do not trust such people. The best writing desks have glorious windows, so much better to stare out of, views upon which not to gaze would be a betrayal, scenes far finer than the grubby page in front of the writer's eyes. My huge window looked out over the river, the other part of the city stacked up on its far bank, the university just visible at the tip of the hill. The large desk, the one I carefully set my things on, was neatly tucked up by the window, flush with the sill.

I did not mention that there was one thing already in place on the desk, a possession of the previous tenant, I assumed. I did not clear it away but merely moved it to one side to allow my objects their space, because it was a typewriter. Those of you who have read *The Biographical Dictionary* will know about the centrality of this once-humble, now-forgotten machine to many writers of the last century, so the presence of one here was most welcoming. Moreover, this was not just any old typewriter, but a late-fifties Hermes 3000. While many would argue for the Olivetti Lettera 22 as the apotheosis of the composing machine, there *is* something about a Hermes: those lovely post-Deco curves, functional yet sensual, Swiss precision over Italian flirtiness, its pleasing heft allowing it to sit as firmly and patiently as an old dog wherever it is placed, the austere grey metal with its hint of sea green, redolent of an Alpine lake on a winter's day. But not just that, no—it is the name. *Hermes*: god of transitions and boundaries, effortlessly shifting between the mortal and divine worlds, trickster, conductor of souls into the afterlife.

The large room was lined with bookshelves, mostly seemingly emptied in haste, only a few lagging volumes slumped here and there. I looked, of course: Enoch Soames's *Negations*, a couple by Vilém Vok, Silas Flannery's *In a Network of Lines That Enlace*. Just a few hours previously I had declared "We have all committed crimes, however large or small, and we shall all face our retribution for them," and it now seemed that my minor misdemeanours had retributed me well, for once. I deserved a celebratory drink.

I swept down the stairs (for these were stairs that one could only *sweep* down), headed out of the door and turned toward my café of the chequered floor, wooden tables and questioning sign, but then realised that I was following the same route as if from the hotel, and that from here I could just as easily turn right and head around a different way, and it is always good to vary one's route.

It was about this time, I think, that I began to have the strange idea that I was being followed. Or rather, if it is possible, I wasn't being followed as much as I was being *preceded*. On my many walks through the city at odd times of day or night, I had often had the sensation not of footsteps behind me, of a shadowy character disappearing just as I turned to look, but of such footsteps and such a shadow just *ahead* of me. Of course, in a busy city, completely empty streets were a rarity, so it should be no surprise should someone be walking the same route as I. And yet, I was rarely following a route: I was merely wandering. I tend to observance, I like to think of myself as someone who notices things, but it was only now, after several weeks in the city, that this strange occurrence became real to me. On each one of my walks, there had always been a character, hardly defined, neither male nor female, not shadowy as much as simply evanescent who was always some distance ahead of me, often turning into a sidestreet only to reappear the same distance ahead of me sometime later. The figure wasn't leading me, because I often randomly changed my chosen path, but it would always show up again.

And so it was on that day. I had scarcely stepped outside of my new home when the figure appeared, heading the same direction as I was, only on the other side of the street. Though I had not the slightest intention of giving up on my well-deserved drink, a certain wilful obstinacy took me and I turned in the opposite direction (knowing full well either direction led me to my bar) and yet, surely, once I had turned the corner the figure (and while I realise that is a poor description, I am afraid I have no clearer way of describing it) appeared again, ahead of me as ever, still on the opposite side of the street, striding ahead purposefully at the same speed as I strode.

In an attempt to give it the slip, I spotted some iron railings, a small gateway into a small park or garden, the one, surely, which stood between my new home and the old hotel. It is possible that I had passed it many times before and simply never noticed it, or had passed and seen only a locked rusty gate and had not registered it until now, when the gate stood open.

I do not like to trespass. I have respect for other people's privacy. I do not like to go where I am not invited. But what is an open gate if not an invitation?

Later, I'd wonder if the gate had not been left open for me on purpose.

A small plot, overgrown grass almost turning to seed at the top, a wooden bench, its slats worn thin by weather. A few headstones poked their heads above the tall grass. On one, a name only, no dates, no further information:

Maxim Guyavitch

I WONDER WHAT IT is about literary graves. Few have great claim to distinction. Wilde has that remarkable Epstein tomb, of course, and (for my money) outdoes Jim Morrison in the Père Lachaise stakes, but as for other pilgrimage destinations: Shakespeare isn't really worth the schlep to Stratford nor Kerouac to suburban Massachusetts (the stone only calls him "Ti Jean") and I suspect those who go to Ketchum, Idaho, to visit Papa Hemingway are probably few and far between and end up disappointed. At least if you go to Westminster Abbey's Poets' Corner you get to tick a good dozen or so luminaries off your list for the (rather steep) entry price (as long as you're happy with a memorial stone and not necessarily the knowledge of dust, bones and a withered heart beneath the slab). Craig Bennett's ashes were allegedly used to fill ashtrays in a Soho drinking den, providing a good excuse to visit one. Keats and Shelley picked a nice spot, I suppose, under leafy trees in a quiet corner of Rome.

But really, what's the point? We go there, ponder a little on mortality, then head off in search of ice cream. I stood there, looking at Guyavitch's unassuming stone, feeling simultaneously awed and bored, wondering if I needed to contemplate mortality any longer than I usually do.

Really, the books are the best headstones. Ever alive.

I was just about to head off in search of ice cream (or maybe that drink and a good read of Guyavitch) when I was surprised by a fellow grave hunter or park visitor.

"I thought you'd find it here." And there, sitting on the worn bench, the Assistant.

"You knew it was here all along?"

"Oh yes."

"And you didn't think to tell me?"

"I think you mistake me, Doctor. I am not Ana, I am her brother, Oto."

So she had a name. And I had never thought to ask. And a twin brother, too, it seemed.

Or so he'd claim five minutes later as we sat in the ?.

"It's rare, yes. But it happens. There have been only ten cases known to medical history in which identical twins are the opposite sex. Of course, we are not perfectly identical."

Oto looked perfectly identical to Ana. I could not have told them apart, the same upturned crescent moon eyes, the strange thin flatness, as if you could fold them, the comic-book curl of drawn-on black hair, the snag-toothed smile.

"There is a Guyavitch museum too, near here. His study, where he spent his last days, perfectly preserved. I think you will be interested, no? I will show you some time. Don't bother with my sister. She gets confused too easily. We do not speak often. A head too filled with books, I fear." The information should have been of great interest to me, but I could do nothing other than look at Oto and wonder if he really was who he claimed to be, or his sister.

~

I SAT AT my desk, gazing out of the window, idly listening to the piano that drifted through every now and again, rearranging my things, trying to think about the story to tell, the story I was being told, and which book I was going to talk about next. When I realised I was daydreaming about Ana and Oto or Oto and Ana, this strange guide, this unreliable Virgil, I realised what it had to be.

The Vermilion Border by C. P. Franck

Let it start here: a meeting of the eyes. Two lines of sight or distracted glances cross and lock for less than a tenth of a second until, embarrassed or not wanting to seem intrusive, the gaze breaks, the eyes turn away but then within less than another second one viewer or the other, perhaps both, turn back, snagged by the sight, drawn to repeat the moment, to risk embarrassment or intrusiveness or incident, to investigate how much accident there may have been in that tiny connection. Yes, there, let it start there, although maybe it started earlier, maybe it started way back, this hermetic germination, this enigmatic parturition, the murky birth of such a thing. Had we several thousand more pages, hours, days, we could go far back, as far as childhood and its knotted ropes which bind us to our parents and trap us with our siblings, on to teenage fumblings and rejections, the first hurt, the first fall, the first victory, all the social shaping, chiselling, moulding and crushing that makes us who we are. But now we do not have time to go so far: the border is approaching.

So let us start here, even though the point of origin will be ever obscure. And yet, I cannot fathom it and must return to the question: where does it begin? This knowledge, this tacit understanding, this unspoken communication, the giving and accepting of permission on the parts of both parties. And why? Whatever, it is done now. Our two, their gaze now unbroken, lean in.

But even here, we rush (though rush we must) for I have not talked of the anticipation, the tenth of a second that lasts a thousand hours, the moment that surely will live in the memories of these two forever, for however long they should live. (Is this the image, I wonder, that will cloud their minds in their final few seconds on this earth?) The anticipation that is greater than the thing which it anticipates. Heart rate increases, we could note the gentle yet ever more insistent pulsing of a vein on the neck of one, a slight flushing of the skin on the part of the other. A lurch in the stomach even, as muscles in the leg flex and slacken while those in the lower face tighten. The tumescence of lips. Breathing becomes more rapid, paradoxically both deeper and more shallow, more intense, more felt. Breath becomes everything, this moment before breath is exchanged. Pneuma: breath as the soul, the first moment of life, a gift, one to another, given and received.

They can almost taste each other now, one's nostrils flare as if to draw in the scent of the other more powerfully, to own them, to take their odour and steal and keep it for themselves. To know this person so intimately their smell becomes yours.

Almost imperceptibly, one draws back, less than an inch, pauses, tries to hold time, as if knowing nothing will ever be the same again, wanting to keep the moment here, to freeze themselves into a Grecian urn, but it is nothing, they find themselves powerless, drawn in, too far now, too close to the border. Less time than the beat of a rapid heart.

Contact.

And now we are lost. One border has been crossed. Nothing will ever be the same again. The first brush of lip against lip, but feathers at first, the stroke of skin on skin. Senses start working overtime, hearts thump still faster, the intensity, they can feel each other's pulse right here where the body's surface is at its thinnest, tenderest, most delicate. Here, where there is no pigment in the skin so the blood that rushes beneath can be seen.

And what do they see? Indeed, what can they see? Are their eyes open or closed? (And you, reader, what kind of a person are you? Eyes closed, or eyes open? It can make all the difference.) Though I cannot see from where I am now, from where I am watching and telling this story, I imagine one pair of eyes open, the other closed. For such it is between lovers: one sees, the other doesn't. One watches, the other dreams. One looks, the other ignores.

So what does the observer see? The bridge of a nose bearing a tiny scar, a scar which will intrigue them though they will never find out its origin. They see eyes closed, trembling lids giving away the flickering of the eyes beneath, they see cheekbone or forehead, close enough now to trace each individual pore in the loved one's skin. They want to see more, ever more. And the other? The one with their eyes closed? They feel.

They feel the slight touch of down on the upper lip or maybe stubble where a razor has passed too roughly over the lower one. They feel the moisture of the lips, the slightest crack or roughness where they have been burned by sun or parched by wind, but scarcely, because these lips are soft, soft, soft way beyond the imaginings of whatever that little word could ever mean, a downy pillow to fall onto and sleep forever, they are tender, they are moist, damp and warm and the lover wishes to stay there, eternally, in those lips, that mouth.

They feel. They feel love.

And now let us step away. Before it is too late for us, and before we are drawn too far into this world.

Excuse me if I quote at length, but I think it's worth it. Is there such a rapturous passage in English? I have cut a little, but I think you get the idea: yes, C. P. Franck's novel *The Vermilion Border* begins with a passage describing a kiss, a single kiss, which lasts for fifteen pages. It is a tour de force, a bravura performance, a magisterial opening as breath-taking and breath-holding as the kiss itself, although one which has equally enthused and infuriated this short novel's few commentators.

The near-forensic levels of detail combined with its heady rush makes it a kind of intoxicant itself—those long sentences, the repetitions and echoes, the shifting back and forth of perspective, the commingling of those vague pronouns so we are never quite sure who's who. Even though this opening, which forms the entire first chapter of the novel, is fifteen pages long, every time I read it, I want more.

Intriguingly, despite the length of the description, there is no mention made of how long this fictional kiss actually lasts—the length of time it takes us to read it? Possible, but implausible. My last attempt to read it took me over ten minutes, long enough to leave even the most ardent lover seriously sore-lipped. But, then, how long *does* a kiss last? How can we ever know? Have you ever set your watch while having a snog? I should seriously hope not.

Yet it is a question worth asking—I think there is a metaphor here. What a kiss can do to time is what reading can do to time: not necessarily to expand or prolong it, but to dissolve it. This passage is a perfect example of that. We do not know how long the lovers are there, yet the narrator (to whom we shall return, patience!) is there, reminding us of time's winged chariot drawing near. Kissing and reading, perhaps, are attempts to defer death.

Let's go back.

> *They feel love. And we know, we have been taught, we have heard the songs and rhymes and read the books and poems, that this is the most wonderful thing. But not for them. Nothing, nothing can be more dangerous for them, for the train in whose dark and empty corridor they are standing is hurtling now, drawing ever closer to the border.*

It is not death that faces these lovers, then, at least not just yet, but a "border." The narrator makes reference to it on several occasions, the only time we are lifted out of the moment of the text, that endless kiss, and into a wider perspective. Where are they heading, and why is this problematic? This is one of the questions this introduction sets up, yet its answer is ambiguous. The border may quite simply be that of moving from being friends or acquaintances or random strangers to lovers. This, truly, can always be dangerous.

And yet there is more. The skill of this book, of this opening certainly, is the shifting of perspective as we move from the almost-molecular level of the description of the kiss to the zoom out. Only after what feels like an eternity do we learn that the putative lovers are on board a train. And suddenly, then, a different border comes into play.

The corridor where they stand and embrace is impervious to what is happening: what can it know of love? Although it has seen much, although many have passed through its narrow space in the many years it has been in service, a railway carriage is an assemblage of steel and iron and remembers nothing. (But if it could, the stories!) The growing night outside the window unspools at speed, whirring past the impervious lovers, the flat planes on the edge of the city become forest then mountains, as we draw closer to the border. The sky turns orange, then purple, then black. The train speeds, and this is good, they feel they are away now, that no one can have followed them. They, wrapped in their kiss, are alone, isolate, free.

The lovers, it seems, are travelling into danger. But who are they?

This, of course, is the question the reader posits, one of the classic whowherewhenwhatwhyhow sextet, the vital cornerstones of plot, or so the manuals tell us. Armed with the little information we have been given as readers, we construct hypotheses:

They are two people, fleeing from some danger—and yet we are told that it is as they approach the border that they are approaching danger—so perhaps they are ignorantly heading into the future, into a state of danger they cannot yet acknowledge. Perhaps they do not have the right authorisation, the correct visas. Perhaps the states divided by this oncoming "border" are antagonists, at war even. Perhaps one of our lovers is a native of one state, the other of the other. Yet Franck tells us nothing. All we can know is that two people are moving from one state into another: from being acquaintances, or perhaps people who have only just met, into being lovers, of passing from one country into another.

This book, I believe, is all about borders and membranes—to kiss is to cross a border, a kiss itself is a border (kisses always create or confirm or break bonds). The mouth is a border—not only of the body, but one of language. It is the place where the two meet: without lips, no language. I am not going to go down the road of saying this book is all about language, that all books are ultimately about nothing other than language itself—though I believe there is validity in this claim, it can ultimately lead us to a dead end. And there is no dead end in sight, at least not yet, for our two protagonists, now hurtling toward the border, the clock ticking.

Alone, isolate, free. But free of what? They do not know who may be pursuing them, who may be watching. And, though love touches them, is love a freedom?

I quote here from one of the most fascinating passages of the book. But before we look at it in more detail, let us return to our question of "who?" for a moment. One of the many admirable things about the way this book is written is that Franck skilfully manages to avoid ever mentioning the sex of either of the lovers. This, of course, leads us back to this pressing question of the "border." Are the lovers a same-sex couple fleeing persecution? How much of a border, a boundary, a limit is our gender?

One of the reasons I find this book so fascinating is that it constantly refuses to give us backstory, to use that term. We draw what we can from the text, and as readers, bring much to bear on it, using our knowledge of the situations the characters are in, of the films we have seen and other stories we may have heard and read. Even though there is little physical description in *The Vermilion Border*, I find I can visualise it perfectly. Maybe, its detractors might say, this is because of its excessive dependence on certain stock tropes, clichés even, but I feel there is more to it than that. Franck is clearly a writer of technical skill and precision, and is doing this on purpose. We are all lovers, even the loveless; we are all in danger. We are all too close to the border.

The sparse yet careful hints of previous lives are dotted in among the rapturous whirl of osculation; there is background here if we look carefully enough. For what kiss is ever the first one? When we kiss, do we not kiss all of our previous lovers? Then there is also the occasional reach out to you—the reader—making you complicit, too. No story can be private, it says: we are all voyeurs.

Yes, someone is watching. As they approach the border, the narrator makes himself physical—even though this is an intense and intimate moment between the putative lovers, perhaps it is not so private after all, we realise, as there is clearly a *third* who is telling this story, a third whose identity is slowly revealed and unravelled through the course of the book.

> *I can wait no longer, loathe as I am to do so, I must interrupt. I should leave them in their peace forever, let them continue, let them fly through the border in their blissful ignorance or guilty shadows. Perhaps they would never know better. But it cannot be: time comes for us all, and I have my work to do.*

Again, our "who?" question: Who is this man? (And yes, I assume it to be a man—even though again a gender is never marked, I feel this gaze is a male one. You may disagree—I'd be interested to know why.)

I slide open the door of my compartment with as much heft as I can manage. Silence is not my weapon. I cough loudly and stamp my boots on the floor to make them heard above the roar of the train as it heads into yet another tunnel. I approach.

As we have by now understood, speed is not the method of this book. Although we are constantly made aware of the speeding train and the rapidly encroaching border, the prose moves glacially, splitting each moment into atoms and observing each one.

At first we believe the narrator to be a ticket inspector, of course — who else would it be on such a train? But then there are hints that he is something more, a customs official or border guard, come to ask for passports, visas or identity papers. There follows a magisterial passage, a meditation on the futility of such documentation, *for what chit of paper, what docket no matter how countersigned and rubber-stamped could ever define who we are?* he asks.

But then maybe he is not even this. As his progress along the corridor toward the still blissfully entwined and apparently unaware lovers continues, we suspect he may be more: an agent of some kind, private or public, charged with a mission of finding just these two people. Maybe he is a benevolent spirit, sent to warn them of the danger into which they are hurtling, or perhaps something darker, one sent to arrest them for their transgression. But more than this: as he observes, getting ever closer, we grow certain that this man knows at least one of the couple. Is he their partner, husband, driven by jealousy? Or even more sinister, a stalker who has seen his prey taken from him?

Our own border draws close, I see, time comes for us too, so I shall not try to answer these questions here, but leave them for you — dear reader — to find alone.

As I have said, *The Vermilion Border* (its title refers to the zone where the lip ends and the skin around begins, an indefinable border) is a book replete with delicious ambiguity and a precise unknowing (if such a thing is possible) and thus reflects its core theme: love itself.

Often, using our knowledge of the author can help us to orient ourselves as readers, it can give us some grist to bring to the mill of interpretation, yet in this case—as in several, sadly, that we look at during this lecture course—we know very little of C. P. Franck. In keeping with the book, we do not know if Franck is male or female, or of what nationality. The book was first published in 1973, and to me has a feel of the later Cold War era which, together with the author's name, suggests someone with a knowledge of Europe, or there again, perhaps merely that most useful of writerly qualities, an incisive imagination.

However, while no translator is credited anywhere, during that opening passage there is, it seems to me, some punning or assonance on the words "eyelid," "lips," "word" and "language" which make me think that perhaps Franck was a speaker of Spanish or Italian: *parpado, labios, palabra, idioma* in the former, *palpebra, labbra, parola, lingua* in the latter. *Lingua* can mean both *language* and *tongue*: two of the book's principal obsessions. Perhaps it is not Eastern Europe then, but some other border Franck has in mind? It matters little, the ambiguity is clearly the important thing. The book's curious prose, that syntax, sometimes sinuous and supple, sometimes awkwardly stretched, the reaching for a dozen words when sometimes, as satiated readers, we may feel as if one will suffice, those incredibly long sentences and longer paragraphs, the blocks of text on the page all bring to mind other writers who I suspect have avidly consumed the book. I occasionally suspect that a nameless translator did an excellent job, and lament not being able to read the book in its original language.

To our other permanent question: If *The Vermilion Border* is such a fascinating book, why then has it been so comprehensively forgotten?

Here, aside from our usual answers, I would suggest another one. This book is a work of romance fiction. This is not a spy novel, not a crime novel, not a thriller. Nor is it a complex meditation on the nature of identity. It is a love story. Romance fiction has a hard time— probably justly—but what love story is not also a story of spies, of crimes, of thrills? And of identity, its loss and redefinition? What love story is not a story about borders and their transgression? In short, what story is not a love story? All books are about love, somewhere. What else is there to write about? What makes us, after all?

I would say more than that. Vagaries of genre modishness aside, I think this book has never been better known because of one of the most powerful, dangerous, destructive and politically subversive forces we know of: that of love.

That the personal is political, that desire is danger zone is far from being a new idea, yet it is one that is true despite its ubiquity, and it is one that is beautifully handled in this book.

Love is terrifying because it means losing the border. To love you have to give away or give up a part of yourself, to redefine who you are, to think of where you end and someone else begins. Love is terrifying because it means losing part of your identity (as—you will find—happens in the book). There is thrill and danger in a kiss, in crossing a frontier, in moving from one state into another, but love, love is more than that.

The Vermilion Border is a short book, scarcely even a novella, but it is nevertheless a powerful, blinding, passionate one. Some critics have found the ending disappointing, but surely—this is the point. "*Love is open, ever unfolding, ever becoming*" writes Franck, as ever teetering on the void between profundity, beauty and banality. (And

yes, banality must play its role too, for so much of love *is* banal—
think of the impossibility of saying "I love you.")

So again, as the book draws to its end, the heft of it thinning in
our right hand, we ask the question, Who are they, these lovers?

We do not know, maybe we never will.

Although this is a lecture, not a review or a teaser trailer, I am
loathe to reveal the ending of the story, its resolution, its climax. For
how does love end? Perhaps, let us hope, it never does.

Thank you.

IT WAS A good ending, I'd thought, slightly let down by the early drift of students to the door as the lecture hour ended. (And there had been fewer attendees than the week before: they'd be putting me in a smaller theatre soon.) The Profesora was one of the leavers, not bothering to deliver her verdict personally but merely leaving a note with its scowl inbuilt. *You will be with us next week. You will converse with Eminent Writer. Taxi will bring you. Spend your days like fox in the hen yard. Onward!*

I SPENT THE NEXT week trying to be little bothered by the Profesora, though I did miss Ana (or Oto) who had sat beside her employer for the duration of the lecture with her customary air of bemusement, then left without giving me the chance to talk to her. I had wanted to ask if she really had a name, and if it was indeed Ana. And did she really have a somewhat morbid twin brother? I wondered how I had been so foolish and impolite as not to enquire. Talking about *The Vermilion Border* had had its effect, it seemed.

My notebook holds no record of that week, and my memory fails, so I assume it was spent quietly, trying to catch up on some reading or simply watching the days shrink. I idly hoped Ana would show up, but she didn't.

Time passed, whatever.

A few days later, however, I do remember returning from the ? after a long lunch to find Jan waiting for me outside my apartment with a huge grin on his face. I'd pleasantly forgotten about the Profesora's threat of dinner with the Eminent Writer.

"You're early," I said, pointing at my watch. He didn't say anything, but once again gestured me to the back of his cab.

"New stock." He grinned. The same shabby boxes sat in the opened boot, holding what initially looked like the same books, all broken spines, mildew and sadness. Not wanting to seem rude, however, I looked a little more closely. A garish orange cover poked my eye and I was amazed to see *Flenge's Dictum* there. This thing, so rare to find in its full form, was a nasty little book with a pernicious reputation which really shouldn't belong anywhere (although if it did have to exist, shoved into the back of a dodgy taxi might be the best place for it). I was curious but didn't touch it, intrigued enough to carry on looking. It was worth it: a copy of Harry Sibelius's unreadable, but nonetheless fascinating *The True Son of Job* was wedged between an obscure medical tract and something in a language I didn't even recognise. I took it, and handed Jan a fake note. I didn't think he'd mind.

"Where'd you get this from?" I asked.

"Contacts," he said. "I can find anything you need. You ask!" I thought about the things I needed, and my mind voided itself. What I needed was time to think.

"I'll need some time to change for dinner," I said.

"Is OK," he replied, "I wait." I should have invited him up for a cup of tea, I know, but I really couldn't be doing with him. I hoped I had already gained at least a slight reputation for being rude and didn't particularly want to lose it. Such a thing can be useful from time to time.

Jan didn't seem bothered when I came back down a couple of hours later, having failed to change but having had a bit of a read instead. He'd engaged a random passerby in a lively discussion about a topic which would remain obscure to me as he swiftly urged me into the Lada-like to chug off to meet the Eminent Writer. I was glad, at least, that the Profesora hadn't trusted me to get there under my own steam and not for the first time had to admit her acuity. I was not at my best, having had a longer lunch than was strictly necessary, and disliking formal dinners with an intensity.

"So who are your contacts, Jan?" I asked, but he responded

only by putting his foot even further down onto the pedal, and my inquiries were lost when I realised I had managed to slam the car door with my coat still poking out. I motioned to Jan to stop but he seemed oblivious, so by the time we arrived in Revolution Square (or maybe Liberation Square, my attention had failed) the corner of the old thing was mud-spattered and worn even more ragged than it had been.

The Profesora (in a Jean Arp design this evening) stood outside the restaurant, smoking.

"You are late, but matter not. No one has missed you."

The gathering sat at a high table, the kind that the Eminent Writer was presumably well familiar with. As I walked in they all seemed as if painted on the walls of a convent, an enigmatic empty seat left by the painter. I was almost ashamed to shamble up late, drape my tatty coat over the back of the empty chair and attempt uneasy discourse.

I have already mentioned my failings as a conversationalist. I find formal dinners where I am expected to be witty, sharp and informed decidedly trying. I prefer to drink in back bars with people who remain unimpressed by the sound of names dropping. To cover up for my social awkwardness I have a tendency to drink too much. Occasions such as this, where drink is both available and encouraged, are fraught with peril. I poured myself a glass.

I was placed directly opposite the Eminent Writer, who was engaged in conversation with a scraggly leather-jacketed man to her left. The group was completed by some people I had seen flitting around the university corridors, and others completely unknown to me. The distracted philosopher appeared for a moment, then left again without saying a word. I looked around for the Professor, but could not see him anywhere.

"Here is Professor," said the Profesora when I asked her, jerking her head toward the scraggly man across from her, still boring the Eminent Writer. I was confused.

"No," I said, "I mean the *other* Professor. *Our* Professor."

"Yes, this man. Head of Department. Professor. Our Professor." An intense scowl, a real hundred-volt one, one which clearly meant *shut the fuck up.* I upped the fuck shut and said nothing else, placing the mystery at the back of my rapidly filling mental storage cabinet of things I wasn't supposed to know for no apparent reason.

I was glad for the man though, whoever he was. He was holding the Eminent Writer in a full nelson of intense discussion on the figure of the author in contemporary society. The Eminent Writer looked seriously bored, in mild pain and utterly unable to escape. I admit I took a degree of pleasure in her discomfort: those who write dull books should be made to suffer at some point. And at least I wasn't having to entertain her.

Meanwhile, we were pelted with local delicacies, the Profesora talking us through the *kroetzen* and *blunchnertort,* down to the details of exactly where, when and how the pig in the *porcsuppe* had been slaughtered, and what uses made of its blood, as well as the precise details of the substance she called "farm cheese," made by leaving milk to curdle in a warm place for up to three weeks. It was all rather delicious, I must say, and I passed the evening avoiding conversation by stuffing my face and drinking too much.

That is, until the moment I saw Professor Two momentarily lose his grasp as he engaged with a hambone dredged from the bottom of his soup bowl. The Eminent Writer seized her moment.

"And what do *you* do?"

For some reason I have never quite understood, when faced

with such a worn question, I often feel compelled to lie. Cruel assemblages of words such as "structural narrative and engagement engineer" and "lexical interface manager" flashed through my mind yet never, fortunately, reached my tongue. I think it was the sad bags that sulked at the corners of her mouth, the way her meringue of hair had begun to wilt or the pleading desperation in her eyes that drew me into dull truth.

I shouldn't have bothered, as the Eminent Writer had ceased listening to me before I had even finished speaking. Such, so often, is the power of truth.

It mattered little as by now Professor Two had discarded the gnawed bone and had reengaged the Eminent Writer with a diatribe on the invalidity of poetry in contemporary culture, at the same time smothering his lips with the rank cheese.

"Last man, not Professor. This man, Professor," the Profesora explained, invoking a conspiratorial hush. "I'm sorry I didn't say the truth, but chicken in the pigsty. Complicated, long story. I will tell you one day." I could see this man as her lover more easily: all scrag and tousle, hair, beard (now flecked with slimy cheese and meatish oil), leather jacket not so much distressed as undergoing a complete nervous breakdown. Clearly someone who wanted to be Bernard-Henri Lévy but came off more a thrift store Žižek, a ham actor playing a pompous intellectual in a cheap biopic of a tortured writer.

Momentary observation of the man dropped my guard. I realised both he and the Eminent Writer were looking at me.

"My second novel," said the Eminent Writer, "*The Lens Grinder's Housekeeper.* It was little read, but I'm sure you know it."

I have just mentioned how easy I find it to fabricate when it is not necessary, and yet how much more difficult to tell the truth when the truth is unwelcome. I could put it down to the wooze caused by the drink and rich food, but that would be disingenuous.

Why do we pretend to have read books we haven't?

There is surely no shame. A million new books appear every year and we cannot possibly have enough time to have read them all. And there are so many competing demands, after all: I need time to stare out of the window, idly look at newspapers and smoke cigarettes. Do we so desperately need to stay modish, to have a voice in the cultural conversation? Entire other books have been written telling us how to pretend to have read those we have not. I do not hold with these. I do not lack confidence: I am proud to say I have not read certain things. The unread, after all, still contains its infinite promise.

And yet, and yet, and yet: the words escaped me.

Oh mouth mouth mouth.

Oh drink drink drink.

Oh books. Books books books. There are too many of you. I love you but you overwhelm me. I just need some space sometimes, that's all.

All of us have that guilty pile: the ones we genuinely want to, the ones we think we ought to, the ones we've tried and promised to return to. It grows ever bigger: books proliferate, multiply, swarm, breed each other, parthenogenerate like those strange plants or rare insects which reproduce without sex. Or perhaps books *do* have sex? Quietly, when we aren't looking, making no fuss and leaving little mess but spawning rapidly.

(I realise I may be contributing to this problem, the production of ever more volumes, but I would argue that my work is an attempt to recuperate, to save those that are already there rather than generate more. I have produced books that are not barren, but which respect strained shelves and straitened pockets.)

So I lied.

It was a poor move, of course. I had extended the limbo of potential embarrassment, the void of having and not having read the book, entered the labyrinth of obfuscation in a desperate attempt to avoid the bitter truth. The Eminent Writer seemed keen to point out it was the complex construction of her second novel that had led to its undeserved neglect but fortunately, before I could be carefully examined about the tricksy narrative structure of *The Lens Grinder's Housekeeper* and plummeted headlong into the abyss of excuse, the conversation shifted to the impossibility of second novels, their inevitable disappointment. I sensed my chance to escape being exposed as a fraud.

"What about Guyavitch? I mean, he never wrote a novel at all, not even an entire book."

"Who?"

He's not so well-known, of course, that I know, but I was somewhat disappointed that the Eminent Writer hadn't heard of him, given that an intimate understanding of world literature was one of the points she managed to trade herself on. But the "who?" also came from the Professor, supposedly an expert. It mattered little, I was oiled enough to deliver my spiel on Guyavitch's greatness anyhow, deeply impressing the Eminent Writer (who, despite everything, I wanted to impress. How feeble I am!) and distracting from the point Eminent Writer kept on wanting to make, bringing up the question of her neglected second novel at each turn or pause in my flow, which by now was proud, strong and confident. The looks on the faces of both Professor Two and the Eminent Writer clearly stated they were impressed, though probably by the quantity I had drunk rather than by the level of my erudition on an obscure central European writer.

I knew when I'd had too much, and I'd had too much. I got up and politely tried to take my leave but the room wouldn't stay upright. I grabbed at my chair for support only to find that the coat I had slung over its back had vanished. I marched off with as much dignity as I could muster.

The gravity of the coat's disappearance didn't hit me at the time, until I realised quite how bloody freezing it was when I got outside. Jan inevitably wasn't there, so I had to walk home, too, equally inevitably getting lost several times in the process. I was doubly annoyed as I had already managed to secrete a bottle of Zapovit in my coat pocket for the trip home, which I now had to make alone, on foot and bottle-less. I hoped the thief choked on it.

I N HIS 1769 *An Essay on Diseases Incident to Literary and Sedentary Persons*, Samuel Tissot warned that "the devourers of books, who exhaust themselves only by reading, should desist as soon as they find their comprehension more than commonly slow, their sight moaty and dimmish, or their eyes hot and watery." When I woke up the next morning, I feared it may have been too late, though it may not have been only books that had made me feel so ill.

There is a literature of illness. The subject has already been discussed in the case of Ellery Fortescue,[6] and there is also *The Magic Mountain*, pretty much all of Proust, Virginia Woolf's wonderful essay, and no great writer truly gets to be considered so unless they've done the whole consumption thing. As Woolf says, it is "strange indeed that illness has not taken its place with love, battle, and jealousy among the prime themes of literature." (And yet, rather than the literature of illness, maybe it is better to talk of the illness of literature: as Fortescue's case shows, it can be the very act of writing or reading itself which is the problem. Language, as Burroughs pointed out, is a virus, after all.)

The literature of illness, however, deals with the grand malaise rather than the daily complaint. Little twinges, dull aches, dicky tummies, bowels over-loose or over-tight, itchy rashes or

_____

[6] See *BDLF*, entry no. 10.

odd pimples: no one wants to read of the sheer banality of most diseases. What may, on the other hand, be far more interesting is the hallucinatory stage of illness. Even a minor affliction can pass through a feverish stage, when lights become brighter, sound intensifies, whispers sound like roars, the skin becomes a membrane of pain, every follicle of the scalp a minute receptor of fever. Thoughts run out of control, become their own leering masters. All food is vile. Every disgusting thing you have ever seen, thought or done leaps to mind. Attempts to think beautiful thoughts are doomed.

It was in such a state that I found myself that morning. Every car passing outside was a monster coming to take me away. The faces of the Professor and the Eminent Writer leered at me. Even the thought of weak tea made my stomach hurl in revolt. I should have tried to use the experience, I thought dully, take it as Keats had, use this febrile stage and make myself one with the pain of all the universe. Instead, all I could do was concentrate hard on not slamming my head against the porcelain as I threw the contents of my stomach into the toilet bowl.

"It is an overhang," the Profesora said when she called later that morning. "*Veersuppe* and *krepfen* never poison anyone. Restorative food." No, Profesora, it is not an overhang, nor even a hangover, I wanted to say. Hangovers I am intimately acquainted with. I know hangovers very, very well. This was no hangover. That morning, I suffered none of the fuzziness of the head and slowness of thought, nor the dull cloud of thunderous pain hanging behind my eyes, the looming existential dread, the sense of regret for everything I had ever done and would ever do, the dull stirrings of grubby desire, the inexplicable dirt under my fingernails, the desire to sleep interrupted by the impossibility of the same act, the temptation of another drink to take the edge off this intolerable condition. There was none of the insatiable desire for carbohydrates liberally garnished with fat and spices. Instead, I had only an intense revulsion for food of any kind and a violent commotion in my lower gut.

I never got a chance to discuss the finer points of alcohol v. food poisoning with her, though, because as it turned out, however bad the poisoning was for me, it had been much worse for the Eminent Writer, who had unfortunately died.

The Profesora calmly informed me that I would have to take over the forthcoming public debate with Important Literature Critic Marcel Mannbrotz.

I drank water, hoping I could keep it down. I went back to bed. I tried to sleep but could not, so tried not to think of the next lecture. Overall, I suspect I had slept badly throughout, for I remember little of the night that was not mare.

This, however, was appropriate, given the book I had chosen and the notes I had clasped under my arm as—but a day after I had apparently cheated the Reaper—I tremblingly made my way to the lectern. Would near-death silence me? Oh no, reader, I am made of sterner stuff.

The Mystery of the Phantom Train
by E. J. Scrowl

The morning broke bright and clear as Shrove set out, his boots clattering on the frostbitten ground. A good walk would blow away some of the previous night's cobwebs. The bad dreams had come with him, it seemed, and he was determined that the cold upland air would sweep them out.

He had arrived in Moreton-in-the-Moor late last night, the train dropping him at a deserted station at an ungodly hour. He'd been the only passenger by then, the others having long since alighted, and as the carriages had moved on through the darkness, he had found himself wondering why he'd chosen to come to such a godforsaken spot. Yet this morning, the memory of his lonely arrival and his curt welcome at the town's only boarding house seemed very distant.

Yes, he remembered why he'd come here, after all. Thomas Shrove, now aged 50, had come to this bracing hamlet to begin his life again. As he passed through the town's few streets and out into the open countryside, he did indeed feel his past fall from him. Here, he thought, here he could

be a new man, the man he was supposed to be, the man he
could have been all along. If only, he thought, he could leave
everything else behind.

Of course, he doesn't manage to do this—what story would we have
if he did? The very setup announces its own decline. What we do
have is a spook story, far more "phantom" than "mystery," clearly
declared to us by the book's somewhat garish cover (its only edition[7]
shows a spectral locomotive ploughing through a deep ravine popu-
lated by grasping anthropomorphous trees, heading toward a mysterious light). If we are familiar with our genre signifiers, our scene
is set immediately.

We rapidly get further into the story as Shrove attempts to walk
further from it. His morning walk out onto the heathland of this
lonely place (possibly somewhere in the English northeast, though
its precise location is never fully revealed) spins him inevitably back
into the memories that he is trying to escape. These are triggered
by two events in particular.

Firstly, the sight of a train speeding through the lowlands beneath
him—or rather, not the sight of a train as such, but the screech and
puff of a train, its only visible sign a plume of smoke rising from the
valley below. He tries to ignore it, ostensibly because the irruption of
such modern engineering into his rural idyll is discomfiting. Yet there
may be more. Trains, it seems, are unpleasant things for Thomas
Shrove, always ready to transport him back to a place where he seems
unwilling to travel. The image grows more eerie as he then comes
across a small village in the moor, nothing more than a closed-up
church, a few grim houses and an inn. He enters the last, in search
of food and company (his ideal solitude already proving just a little

---

[7] Bendrix & Bazakbal, 1934.

more than he is comfortable with) and finds little of either: a stale ham roll, a taciturn barkeeper and a dog. The beer is flat, warm and watery. No welcoming fire is lit in the grate. Shrove attempts to make the best of the situation by engaging in conversation, commenting to the barkeeper that he had seen a train passing in the valley below. The barkeeper shakes his head. *No train hereabouts. There was talk of one when my grandfather were a nipper, but nowt ever come of it.*

Shrove thinks little of it, trusting his senses more than a miserable northern publican, drinks up and leaves.

Then comes the second thing. As he is heading back to his lonely boardinghouse in the meagre town, he sees a figure ahead of him, on the ridge of a hill under which he is passing. He calls out to the figure, who he believes to be a woman, though he cannot be sure; but though the figure turns, he can discern no face, and as he gets closer the figure disappears. He cannot explain the disappearance, he is in open countryside, not so much as a tree to vanish behind. No one could have got so distant as to be no longer visible in the time it took him to walk up the hill to find his quarry. On this occasion, he allows himself a slight mistrust of his senses, assuring himself it could have been a trick of the light, some strange effect caused by wind and shadow, perhaps, and certainly there was no one there.

Yet the doubt persists, of course, as persist it must, as he returns from his circular walk to find himself feeling he is being followed, though every time he turns he is aware of nothing more than a character vanishing from sight, as though it existed only in his peripheral vision and could never really be seen.

He eventually returns to his lodging that evening, exhausted and not in the frame of mind he had set out in, but worries little about it. It will take time, he assures himself, as he sits down to a dinner of mutton stew and a half bottle of gritty claret, before heading into a deep and thankfully dreamless sleep.

So, by this point we've come a fair way through the first part of the book. Scrowl then keeps the narration cantering along at a fair chug, idling over details only as far as they are necessary (the descriptions of light on the landscape are notable, how in such a solid place, the land little more than rock and rain and scrubby grass, everything can still seem so transient, so light, so shifting). We are familiar with the genre, Scrowl assumes, and therefore the author can carry us along rapidly.

The next day Shrove sets out again, and (foolishly) having no map, he decides to do the same walk as yesterday, though this time in the reverse direction. Of course, he gets horribly lost: seen from this reverse perspective everything is completely different. Though he tells himself that he is perfectly at home in cities of any size, the shifting topography of this landscape baffles him continually. The low fields he remembers have become high plains, the gentle climbs steep gradients. He continually sees figures, sometimes alone, sometimes in couples or small groups making their way across the fields, but every time he attempts to call to them, they disappear. As the light begins to fade (so early this time of year, so far north), Shrove finds himself cold, wet, lost and alone. He eventually sees lights, moves toward them, though they move as he does, and by the end he is running, trying to catch a village that is steaming away at the same pace as he is. And then he finds it. At first he thinks it is the same small town he had lunched in the previous day, but then notices everything is slightly different. A generous barmaid stands behind the counter, a pint of foaming ale awaits him, the dog leaps up and licks his hand, recognising a friend. He sits, breathes and relaxes, warmed by the roaring fire in the hearth. He scans the books propped on the mantel above the fireplace: a few guides to the area, a tattered collection of verse and a few popular novels. One catches his eye. Its title? *The Train of the Mystery Phantom.*

(At this point, certain readers may have a desire to hurl the novel as far across the room as they can muster. Others, however, may be amused, intrigued, provoked. I hope, for all our sakes, that we are among the latter group. Scrowl was writing in the early 1930s, let us remember, long before the word "postmodern" had even been conceived, and the word "tricksy" was used only to describe card players. There are neither of those potentially annoying qualities here, only a skilled writer working very cleverly with genre constraints and reader expectations.)

Let us turn back to poor Shrove, who, of course, begins to read.

The Train of the Mystery Phantom turns out to be a strange book, one which Shrove wants to dismiss, yet is compelled to keep reading. Published in the early Edwardian era, we are told (and therefore some thirty years before Shrove's story is taking place), the book posits itself as a scientific piece of work on investigation into the spirit world. It begins with a long theoretical introduction (including many diagrams and equations) in which the author (one Norton Conyers) dismisses séances and suchlike as hokey fakery, while accepting other paranormal phenomena as scientifically reasonable, potentially rational and therefore explicable, explorable and quantifiable. He intends to use the nascent media of photography and radio transmission to verify his findings, and to make contact with other dimensions.

Conyers, an English aristocrat with a penchant for the paranormal, takes as his case the mysterious reported sightings of a train passing through a valley in Hexhamshire, a place where no train line had ever been laid.

The second part of his book, as Shrove finds out, details his mission to this remote area, along with a team of spectographers and scientific-spiritualists, not to dispel popular myth, but to find whatever substance there is in it.

Shrove discreetly slips the book into the folds of his capacious overcoat, bids the hostelry good night and makes his way back to his own lodgings (which this time he fortunately manages to find without trouble), and sits up for the rest of the night reading *The Train of the Mystery Phantom*. His late reading is intense, disturbed only by the occasional sounds of rain, steam and the hiss and screech of speed which leak in through his draughty window.

He wakes early the next morning, another bright, cold day, and decides on a course of action of his own. He will use Conyers's methods to solve his own questions. Who was the figure he saw on the ridge? And why did she seem so familiar? And, yes, what *is* it about that bloody train?

The rest of the narrative flickers between Shrove's continual reading and re-reading of Conyers's book and his own experiences in the small, strange town. It reaches the point where the two merge, and the reader is often left unanchored, never quite sure if they are reading what Shrove is reading, or what he is experiencing, or quite which of the two we are being told. Shrove's grasp on any objective reality seems to slip along with our narrative moorings as he gathers around him the tools he can: a typewriter, which he connects to the basic main electricity supply; a compass, which he attempts to link to the rudimentary telephone network, believing its disembodied voices will then point him toward unexplored locations; a gramophone player, which he tries to use in reverse, to record rather than replay sound. All these things, he believes, will summon spirits. He attempts to prove the existence of ghosts by complex mathematical formulae (which Scrowl, thankfully, spares us). Of course, we intuit that he is going mad, but also that his madness is entirely logical and reasonable.

As we follow his growing obsession, his story is traced out for us: the woman he last saw boarding a train—a lover, perhaps—who may have been leaving him, or may have been killed in a tragic accident.

He seems to have been obscurely implicated in or responsible for her death or disappearance, yet nothing has been said, hence his own choice to disappear. The detail is left tantalisingly yet pleasingly open. We see that he is, unknown even to himself, attempting to bring her back, believing her a passenger on the ghostly train that moves by night through this desolate land.

The Mystery of the Phantom Train ends as such a book should begin: with the stipulation of an enigma. We see Shrove set out one morning, as ever, with his trusty tools and notebooks shoved into the pockets of his coat, but we do not see him again for several days. An alarm is put out; we end with a curt police report. A body fitting his description has been found. No possessions other than a shabby overcoat containing the manuscript of a rambling book entitled *The Phantom of the Mystery Train*.

~

So why did this fascinating book disappear? There are a few answers to this, some of them disappointingly obvious.

Firstly, despite its aforementioned postmodern playfulness, it is a book decidedly of its era. Despite the rattling pace of its plot, the prose, to be honest, often plods with a tread as leaden as that of Shrove himself in his heavy boots on the sodden moorland. Scrowl, I imagine, hadn't read enough M. R. James but had read too many of his many substandard imitators. But while I say that it is a book of its era, it is also one that is both slightly too late and slightly too early. By the 1930s the era of the great ghost story was over (or at least going through a fallow phase, having yet to be reinvented), as crime took over as genre of choice.

Far from being at the fag-end of one tradition, it is better seen as being at the beginning of a new one. With its odd emphasis on technology and its disfigurements, it suggests a kind of steampunk J. G. Ballard.

Then, of course, there is the book-within-the-book, a device which may look potentially hackneyed today, but seemed so radical as to be off-putting for contemporary readers: the book sold little, and Scrowl returned to writing moderately successful cosy crime stories. The use of the device is, however, far from hackneyed in this book, and thus I have chosen to lecture on it today. In *The Mystery of the Phantom Train* readers find themselves continually wrong-footed, expecting the path to lead one way, then finding it turns in another. It is a book which, as we noted, begins as a solid, workaday supernatural thriller, steaming toward an improbable and disappointing dénouement, something involving literal smoke and mirrors, but then takes a radical swerve into the unknown.

Narrative point of view is consistently undermined or denied. There is nothing so trite or pat as an "unreliable narrator" here: what we have instead is an unreliable *author*, unreliably witnessing the acute grief of a man's utter mental breakdown.

There is one other thing. I had always blithely imagined "E.J." to be Edward John, Edmund Jacob or Eric Jeremy, a minor don, country rector or public school housemaster with an eccentric interest in local history and a fine collection of tweed jackets, but I was very wrong. "E.J." in fact stands for "Elizabeth Jane." Elizabeth Scrowl, as well as running a sideline in crime novels, was also an intrepid traveller and radical socialist who fought with the International Brigades in the Spanish Civil War.

One last thing about this book.

I have long since lost my own copy, one of the few remaining treasures I had from the Paramount Book Exchange on Shudehill in Manchester, and apart from my opening quotation, which I have stored in my notes, everything I have related to you today is based on my memory of the thing and not, I'm afraid, the kind of close re-reading I usually undertake before such a lecture as this one. Though I have tried, I cannot track another copy of the book down anywhere, and have only ever found scarce and fleeting clues as to its very existence.

This is a book which seems to be trying its own very best to disappear, to cease to exist before our eyes, leaving us uncertain as to whether it was a real thing, or merely a memory of one. The book itself is a ghost.

Thank you.

DESPITE A THINNER crowd than usual, the lecture had gone well, I thought, the rapping on desks a pleasing echo of a séance, but I confess I had been considerably thrown off my stride by the appearance of a ghost I recognised only too well. "Speak of ghosts, and they will come," wrote Guyavitch in "Dead Johann." And one had. Not a ghost exactly, I should say, but a revenant, certainly: he'd sat in the second row, making sure he was visible to me, wearing a suspiciously familiar overcoat and a supercilious gaze. I should have expected him sooner.

If I may, I will leave him there for a minute, as the story will take time to tell, and right now the Profesora is regarding me with gimlet-eyed scrutiny.

"Spook story, again. Enough with all these yellow books. We do not have such things in our country. No ghosts, only stories. We are rational people. For such, your lecture not appropriate. Something with more weight next time please."

I wanted to ask her what could have more weight than the questions of life, death and what might come between them that I believe the book raised, but instead merely mumbled an apology and a vague promise to do better next time.

"Though I must say you yourself seem a ghost today," she continued. "So perhaps appropriate after all."

It was true. Though I had recovered from the violent bout of food poisoning, I was still in the convalescent phase, feeling strangely new-born yet faint, as though someone had begun to erase me around the edges but had not quite finished the job.

"Is this perhaps because your protagonist goes walking much, gets lost often, worries he is being followed, and steals books?"

"I'm not sure what you mean."

"Yes you do, Doctor. We all like to find ourselves in books, no?" A strange sound that resembled a laugh came from her throat. "But how much more interesting to find other people, yes?"

"That, Profesora, is very true."

"But no, you are not Mr Shrove of the book, I think," she conceded. "Though pale, you are not a ghost. Not yet, at least. A ghost I think would not drink so much. It is good you drink. Zapovit is a health drink. An all-cure." I understood the Profesora was telling me the amount of the spirit I had drunk on the occasion of the dinner with the Eminent Writer had been enough to kill whatever else it was in the meal that had nearly done for me and had done for the Eminent Writer, but she was too polite to say so. "Have a glass each evening. It is what keeps me hale—even if they try to poison me! Ha! Meanwhile, you have public debate with Important Critic this evening. Forget not, please."

"Will the Professor be there?" I asked, still disappointed that I hadn't managed to capture his undivided attention on the evening of the fateful dinner.

"Ah, I must tell you, the man who was with me that evening, he is not the Professor."

"Not the Professor?"

"No. Not Professor." On top of a bout of near-fatal food poisoning and the ominous reappearance of an old acquaintance, I was now expected to try and process this bolt of information.

"Then who was he?"

"Story longer and twistier than grandmother's noodles. Another time. But real Professor will come to the debate, I think." And before I could ask any further questions or indeed vent any further bafflement or frustration, she was gone.

~

AND NOW I was left alone with my own ghost, the character stretching his ludicrously long legs onto the bench in front of him, a man who had apparently managed to remain invisible to the Profesora.

"So they call you 'Doctor' now, do they?"

"Squattrinato," I finally said, for it was he. "I might've known you'd turn up here."

For those of you who do not know, the figure of Fausto Squattrinato is a confusing one. I first came across him many years ago when I was living in Naples, and since then he has continued to crop up with annoying frequency.

"Getting laid?"

"Fuck off, Fausto."

"Evidently not, then. What happened with . . . ?"

"Fuck off, Fausto."

Squattrinato claims to be a performance artist, and that his entire life is his performance. He is an inveterate liar, has no known source of income and a disturbing habit of appearing when least wanted.

"Nice coat, by the way." He wasn't wrong there, for once. Concerned by the now-explained disappearance of my previous coat, and the consequent likelihood of my freezing to death as the weather turned ever colder, I'd called the restaurant that morning. They assured me I hadn't left it there, but did have one that was almost identical to mine which they would be more than happy to offer me (though missing the bottle of Zapovit and the copy of Alicia Hoyle's *Fear Mantras*). I had picked it up on my way over to deliver the lecture and was pleased to find it had better lining than its predecessor, and bigger pockets too.

I looked at my old one, its capacious pockets now undoubtedly emptied of bottle and book and instead filled by the grubby hands of the self-declared legend.

"It seems you haven't fucked off yet, Fausto."

"Did you hear the Beasleys have re-formed?"

"I'd heard, yeah." One of his projects was an involvement with the shady literary group, the Beasley Collective,[8] but their very existence has been doubted by many, and Squattrinato's claimed links to them were even more doubtful.

"They're after you," he warned me.

"Them and the taxman, then. And several others too."

"Something about royalty payments."

"They think I owe them money?"

"You know what anarchists are like."

"How did you manage to steal my coat?"

"It's not theft, it's reappropriation," he sighed. "How many times do we have to go through this?" It had been one of his favourite discussion topics, this was true. "Anyhow, you're all successful now, aren't you?" he carried on. "I see you've got yourself a new one already."

"Success is relative, Fausto, as you well know. Are you following me, too?"

"Not following, no. Not my style. I was passing through, and heard you were in town. One of my regular stopovers, this place. A city with a fine literary heritage."

"You've never been here before in your life, you lying git," I told him. "And you're looking fat," I added, though in truth he was still rail-skinny.

"Healthy, I'd say. Not like you."

"And what is with that ridiculous beard?"

"Women love it. You should give it a try. Might improve your luck."

---

[8] See *BDLF*, entry no. 3.

"I have no need of luck."

"I strongly doubt that. Shall we go and nick something?"

"Don't you mean 'reappropriate'? Or is it 'recontextualise' now?" Whatever his favoured term, petty pilfering has long been one of Squattrinato's pastimes (and, I suspect, a source of his income), and it is one with which I will have no part, as he well knew.

"Call it what you like. Must be some good bookshops in this town."

~

IT WAS ON our way out of the university that we ran into Ana. She apologised for her absence today, and told me she had some news I might find interesting.

"There is a museum," she said, "for Guyavitch."

"I know," I said. "Your brother told me about it."

"Brother?" she asked. "I don't have a brother."

~

IT WAS AT this point I began to wonder how long I had been ill, and whether the illness that had taken me and which I had blamed on the dangerous food was perhaps only the culminating symptom of something I had been suffering from for much longer. What that ailment may have been I could not say, however, and rapidly dismissed the suggestion. There was nothing new in the fact that I had been having strange dreams (especially frequent, I find, when one is transplanted to a new home in a new country), though the fact that I'd had that feeling of being followed, or rather, anticipated, was an odd one. The strangeness of the fact did not detract from its sense of realness, however, its sense of experiential veracity. There was nothing hallucinatory about what had happened, no matter how strange it had been. Oto had suggested the two were on bad terms, of course, and I took Ana's answer to mean that the terms were perhaps only worse than I had taken them for.

Before I could ask Ana about her twin, however, Squattrinato had seized his moment.

"Guyavitch?" he asked me. "Do you still believe in that guy? I thought he didn't really exist."

"That's nonsense." Aside from the fact that Guyavitch seemed to be controversial in his very birthplace, an idea I was still having trouble getting used to, there is another complicating theory in the whole story. In his book *The Guyavitch Heresy*,[9] Max Gate puts forward the idea that Guyavitch was merely a pseudonym used by multiple writers and editors, and that the man himself never really existed. He was, suggests Gate, a character invented in order to forge the uncreated conscience of a formative nation, one which never eventually managed to congeal.[10] Guyavitch's biography is indeed so chequered and patchwork, so riddled with inconsistencies and lacunae that Gate's theory is certainly a tempting one, but ultimately it holds little water. While I am certain that Guyavitch was a man of many guises, and one with a complex and bitty life, the stylistic unity of the existing stories does not point to many hands. Writers are crafty beings in every sense. They would do much to escape definition.

"Nonsense is a fine art," declared Squattrinato, "and I am a master practitioner of it. When you need a writer, why not

---

[9] William & Wilson, 1982.

[10] The book is written in the mode of a breathless thriller, which sadly does little to advance its intriguing case.

simply make one up? It's the perfect solution, far less messy than having to deal with the real thing." He cracked a grin and I was pleased to be interrupted by an impatient Ana.

"Perhaps a museum will prove it one way or the other," she said. "Would you both like to come?"

An obscure museum dedicated to a lost writer is, of course, one of the few things more tempting than a dusty library or dark bar. I needed no further invitation, and neither did Squattrinato, who, surprisingly, turned out to still have the bottle of Zapovit in his pocket. A few nips kept us warm as we set off on our adventure.

Thirty minutes and several nips later, we were still walking.

"Do you know where you're going?" Fausto asked Ana.

"Not exactly," she replied.

"At least we can't get lost, then."

"It's near a bookshop," she said.

"I thought there were only two bookshops in town," I replied.

"There are."

"We've been to one."

"It's not that one. It's the other one. The Ex-Wife bookshop."

"And do you know where that is?" Scepticism welled in Fausto's voice.

"Vaguely," replied Ana, unconcerned. "I was born here, and I grew up here, but I can never find anything. We natives know something no one else does: the city moves every night, when no one is looking."

Squattrinato was enjoying the walk, the drink, the company of a young woman, but his long legs increased our pace so much we could scarcely keep up with him.

"Like old times, this, isn't it?" He grinned back to me, and he wasn't wrong, but they were times best left behind. Fortunately, the Ex-Wife bookshop appeared before he could go any further, and Ana decided to enquire within.

"It's never easy talking about Guyavitch, but she might know something."

The bookshop-owning ex-couple must have been a strange partnership in their time. We have already seen the Ex-Husband bookshop and heard its story; the Ex-Wife bookshop, on the other hand, evidenced a very different proprietor. Well-polished windows displayed nothing but a couple of overly tasteful abstract prints, pictures for the walls of top-end chain hotels and a small pile of a current glossy-jacketed international bestseller too dull to bother naming.

We went in. We were the only people in there. There was no welcome: customers were not welcome here. Customers, this shop said immediately, are grubby outsiders who have nasty habits. Customers are the kinds of people who do things like remove books from shelves and put them back in the wrong places, ask annoying questions, crease spines. Customers stand around and clutter the place up, reading books without paying for them. Customers sneeze and cough.

The few titles available sat neatly arranged on tiny tables, perfectly displayed. Their covers glistened. They were not to be touched. Everything was to be admired; nothing was to be read. There is a bookshop in Tokyo which only ever has six books in stock at any one time: the stock changes monthly, but there are only ever six titles available. On the rare occasions I have had the chance to visit this shop, the six titles have all been excellent. However, if the proprietor of a shop is not of extremely good taste, having very few books is rarely a good sign. There were no good signs here. This shop was run as a hobby, a showcase, a vanity project. There was no love for the pursuit of a literary ideal or even the earthy matter of print housed in these premises.

A woman with sharp hair appeared and glowered at us. The Ex-Wife. Ana engaged her in what sounded like brittle conversation while Squattrinato and I split up, though the Gorgonian proprietor still managed to keep an eye on each of us. I was sure I heard the word "Guyavitch" uttered with steely disdain and sensed that Ana's investigative attempts were not going well.

I turned out to be wrong: while Ana's questioning had managed to yield some meagre fruit, it was to Fausto and me that the owner seemed to have taken some unfounded exception. I shall not bore the reader with the details of yet another intricate and unfortunate misunderstanding, but suffice to say this was not the place for the likes of people who prefer to wear clothes with large pockets in the backrooms of bookshops, and several minutes later, after the owner had set a particularly bad-tempered mastiff loose on us, we were outside, breathlessly showing each other our spoils.

"I did manage to find something out," said Ana as we ran off down the street. "She claimed never to have heard of Guyavitch, but did say someone kept a room dedicated to a writer in a house near here, in one of the back courtyards."

We scoured the connecting backyards, spaces which extended behind the tenement facades to provide a kind of counter-street. Each led into another, and then another, a maze of disappearing streets leading farther back into what may have once been one enormous building, punctuated only by endless inner yards. There was no sign of a museum.

By now it was getting late, and time to get to the Municipal Theatre for the public debate was running thin. We agreed to return another day, knowing it was unlikely we'd ever find the place, but Squattrinato and I were contented by showing each other the copies of Adeodato Lampustri's *The Carmassi Brothers* and Maurice Bendrix's *The Grave on the Water-Front* which had appeared in the deep pockets of our well-appointed overcoats. Strange, how so often the most unlikely places house the oddest treasures.

T HE *VORTS VILJANDI* Municipal Theatre was neatly
tucked into a corner of the apparently cornerless Liberation Square (or perhaps Revolution Square) and the three of us
barged through its doors with only minutes to go until show-
time, I readily expecting to have to elbow my way through the
eager crowds, or—even better—to be chaperoned through them
while waving graciously and signing autographs as I passed.

Instead, we found the place deserted.

A photocopied piece of paper taped to the main door did
announce the evening's event, but unfortunately still advertised
the Eminent Writer, news of whose sad fate had obviously not
reached the organisers. We walked unchallenged toward the
main hall to find the doors closed and a shabbily attired and
unfriendly assistant concierge telling us that we should be in
the basement theatre. I had no problem with this: I am not one
for great hallways, massive stages, raked banks of seating, stalls
and circles—an intimate space is far more suited to my temper-
ament and my work. The basement theatre, however, turned out
to be more basement than theatre.

Light was scarce, and the audience scarcer than in my lectures. The three people who had shown up sat on plastic seats
which scraped the lino floor every time they shifted. A mop and
bucket were propped on the stage, alongside three more chairs

and a single spotlight, as if waiting for an as yet undiscovered Beckett production.

Of the three people there, two were the Profesora and the Important Critic himself, I assumed, given that he was deep in mutinous conversation with her (I do not apologise for the word "mutinous"—if ever a conversation seemed mutinous, it was theirs). The Professor was to chair the session, and I assumed the third audience member was he. I introduced myself to the sallow young man, who was slumped in the plastic seat swinging a large bunch of keys. He looked at me and shrugged his shoulders.

"Not Professor," said the Profesora. "Technician."

"Oh," I said. "No Professor?"

"No Professor. We do not need Professor. Few people here."

I had thought little about this occasion, as the reader will already know, but at the back of my mind I had visualised the Important Critic interviewing the Eminent Writer, with occasional sage interventions from the Professor, but now it seemed as if it were to be some debate on the state of literature today or literature's role in the global conversation or some other equally worthy and utterly tedious subject in which I held little to no interest whatsoever. It didn't worry me though: romance at short notice was one of my specialities.

The Profesora beckoned to me, ignoring Ana and Fausto.

"This is Important Critic Marcel Mannbrotz," she said. "I'm sure you know his work." I smiled and fortunately resisted the compulsion to lie and merely stayed silent, still smiling, feeling awkward as they both paused, waiting for me to say something.

"A pleasure to meet you," I said, still smiling, ignoring the obvious but determined to resist the impish temptation. They continued to pause; I continued to smile. Mannbrotz was an odd-looking little thing: a small mound of smooth, pink, tender, fleshy fleshiness with large fat wet lips. He was very short with a head the shape of an inverted sparrow's egg—narrow at the bottom and growing larger toward its smooth shining dome. He wore spectacles that only exaggerated his oddness, horn-rimmed and neither perfectly circular nor regularly oval. No beard, but speckled bristles crept around the lower half of his face, seeking refuge under his chin. A starched white shirt was buttoned up to the neck but with no tie, in that curious fashion that gestures to the modish but always seems merely that the wearer has forgotten to put one on.

He extended his hand and I shook it. I will have no part of that macho bullshit that judges a person by the strength of their radial, carpal or digital muscles, but a weak handshake never bodes well. He had a weak handshake.

"A pleasure to meet you, too," he eventually responded. Strange, sometimes, how so much can be discerned in but six words, a cluster of some dozen phonemes. Mannbrotz lingered on each sound, riding the rise-fall inflection of his utterance as if it were a well-mannered thoroughbred cantering over the lower slopes of a lush mountain. The accent he luxuriated in was curiously English-upper-class, despite its occasional local inflection. I wondered how and where he had learnt it, and suspected it may have been through watching straight-to-Netflix low-budgeters shot on a Los Angeles backlot with a solid British character actor as the anonymously evil villain.

I suggested to the Profesora that we might like to wait a little, for latecomers to arrive, but she dismissed my suggestion. To be fair, there were now four or five people seated, apart from Ana and Fausto who had chosen to sit as close to the back as possible, probably to stage an early and unseen exit.

(It wouldn't have been the smallest crowd I'd addressed. I was once invited to talk about *The Biographical Dictionary* at a large bookshop in London, only to find that I'd been double-booked with a fake-Italian celebrity chef. I sat alone at a signing table, contemplating the buttocks of those queueing to have the cook sign their books as they swamped my small and lonely eyrie.)

The three seats on the stage were awkward. I took the one on the left, Mannbrotz the one on the right leaving the largest central chair, the only one with a microphone, presumably intended for the interlocuting Professor, vacant. We looked at each other, still smiling, waiting for our invisible host to begin the proceedings.

Nothing happened.

I looked at Mannbrotz; Mannbrotz looked at me. I smiled; he didn't. His shirt gleamed at me. Light spun off his head. His tiny eyes beaded behind his glasses. We both looked at the empty chair, then he looked at me.

There is a certain type of critic, or sometimes of writer, who has to see everything as a challenge or matter for a debate in which points are to be scored and reputations to be made or won for some non-visible, largely imaginary prize or award. This type of critic is waiting for nonexistent judges to give a points decision in the third round, to spin their chairs or hit their "yes" buzzers, to be called forth. They will seek any chance to obliterate those they regard not as comrades, shoulder-to-shoulder in the same great struggle of the word against the world, but as competitors or rivals jousting for whatever meagre prize they imagine lies at the top of the heap of broken spines and torn pages whose summit they aspire to. Writers and other critics are elbows to be shoved aside by more forcible elbows, targets to be taken out by wit that can aim well and reload quickly, rats to be bashed back down the drainpipe of history by the baseball bat of recondite powers of reference. Jealousy runs hard where the scant rewards of review inches, sales figures and minor prizes run scarce. I have heard critics pour poison, poets talk knife fights.

And as I sat under the light, the empty darkness of the small audience before me, looking at the little mound of glabrous podge now fixed on me, I realised, alas, that Marcel Mannbrotz was one such man.

Even with the notable absence of our interlocutor, I assumed introductions and pleasantries would be the natural opening for such an evening. It was not to be.

"I have read your work, Doctor," said Mannbrotz. "I did not enjoy it."

Needless to say (I hope the reader knows me well enough by this point), I will have no part of this behaviour. I believe in literature as a collaborative adventure, a joint enterprise of reader and writer (and reader-writer and writer-reader). I dislike Pharisees who put us behind them in the queue to follow the light. Books, I believe, are part of the great communality of human experience, our shared heritage and invested future. Literature is vast, welcoming, polyphonic, forgiving. It is so unlike life, and that is perhaps the reason I love it so.

I suspect Mannbrotz would have lambasted me for having such an opinion.

"Even though I have found your work facile, I should like to ask you a few questions about it," he continued, and I wilted.

I am, I confess, not always a rapid thinker. I am more one for slow contemplation— for such reason, I prefer the written word to the spoken one. Words I can look at for ages, move them around on the page, inflect and caress them until they do as close to what I want them to do as possible. The spoken word is out and gone and has done its damage in less than a second. I mistrust it, especially when clouded by anger. So often, those who care are at a disadvantage in such debates, compared with those who do not. That evening, though, it was all I had.

He looked at me, eyes squinting through his spectacles, and began.

"The value of hermeneutics is one which obviates the necessity for a radical, transformative heuristics."

"Was that a question?" I asked.

"More of a conjecture."

"Oh."

Silence.

"Trautmann has written that 'Truth is always laden with its other,'" he continued.

"Indeed."

"You don't know Trautmann?"

"Not personally, I'm afraid."

"'Towards a Reconfiguration of the Axiomatic Paradigm'?"

"No."

"It's a crucial essay. You should read it."

"I'll put it on my list."

"Let's try another tack, then." Mannbrotz sighed theatrically. "Given the acknowledged impossibility of subjectivity, would you say that the Scylla of an ipso-relative position necessarily leads to the Charybdis of aliorelativity?"

"Erm, yes?"

"Hm. My problem, you see, is that your work posits a paradigm in which protasis becomes all too easily confused with apodosis, and on this hinge a range of inchoate corollary statements."

Silence again.

More silence.

"Come, Doctor," he continued. "We are a duumvirate, called upon to deliberate. So let us deliberate."

"I would like to deliberate, but I'm afraid I haven't the foggiest idea what you are talking about."

"Ha! Turnips and swedes, Doctor, turnips and swedes. Or should we say rutabaga and kohlrabi? Ha!"

"Ha! Yes, quite."

"You must be familiar with Szycz's work on the subject?"

"I'm afraid not."

"Bogdan Smith? 'The Impossibility of "Yes"'?"

"Nope."

"You should know it," he sighed. "I'm surprised at such a lack of intellectual curiosity."

Silence again. A little murmuring in the audience. I saw a man enter, the distracted philosopher. I reached for a glass of water, but none had been provided. I wondered if Squattrinato could slip me the bottle of Zapovit, but he was too far away, no doubt glugging on it himself, thoroughly enjoying this shabby spectacle. I shifted in my seat. I'm given to touching my face in situations of stress. I touched my face.

I must point out here that I am absolutely not anti-intellectual. As I have already stated, I will praise those who have had the sap from their veins dried out by difficulty, I will pursue the difficult, I am fascinated by the difficult. Theory is a beautiful thing, and so often better than practice. But what I cannot stand is the wilfully obtuse, the inelegant, the poorly written. Writing badly is a crime. Bad writing is an expression of bad thought. I do not repeat this whole sorry incident to mock those whose work takes them into difficulty, nor those who rightly use the right word in the right place knowing their readership or audience. I am recounting it because I hated Marcel Mannbrotz.

Hours passed, though they were probably only seconds. Someone in the audience coughed. Things took a turn for the worse.

"You probably believe in Guyavitch, don't you?" I was surprised to hear him mentioned, but sensed a possibility of turning the conversation around.

"Well, he is a writer in whom I have some interest, yes." Mannbrotz sniggered. A proper snigger. A sniggerer's snigger.

"Given your evident credence in the nonobjective empiricism of the desert of the hypothesized real, I am hardly surprised. These are, as you may or may not know, strange times in our country, and at such times all kinds of monstrous births become possible. The Guyavitch fallacy, for example, is one that is a popular rumour, a folk hallucination. People make Guyavitch because they want Guyavitch. Indeed, if you had read my work on the subject you would have known this. Let me exemplify," he continued. "You see, I am *not* Marcel Mannbrotz. I look like him in many respects, resemble him, know the man intimately, but I am not him. I am a simulacrum, produced by our expectations of him. I am his avatar, his performing seal, his court jester. I am your projection of Mannbrotz, but not Mannbrotz. The man you see before you is not real."

I wondered if I punched him, how real he'd be.

"Am I clear?" He wasn't, but he was in full flow now. "What are we to do with these writers and these books you so blithely talk of? Where are their works? Where is their reality, their psychological veracity? Who are they if not unlikely assemblages of verbal tics and improbable costumes, repeated tropes and inadequate endings? How facile are your odd obsessions and puerile credence?"

I had nothing to say. I wanted to go home. I didn't even want a drink anymore.

"It's what you call *snark*, isn't it? Isn't it? That is all your work amounts to. Find the spurious lost in order to deny the great their hour, their day. Fiction is done for: the point in our times is not to *imagine* but to *interpret*. For all your searching and rummaging and pilfering, Doctor, there is little or nothing to be found in the margins. Don't go rooting in dusty bookshops. Don't go looking for lost libraries. Stop wasting our time with the petty, stop validating the lost, it is gone, of no use or significance to us now. The dead are dead."

He stood up. I couldn't move. There was a murmur of applause, and we were done.

L
ATER, AFTER WE'D huddled into a corner of the ?, I found myself thinking about verbal tics and improbable costumes and looked at myself, Squattrinato and Ana, and wondered if verbal tics and improbable costumes were not, after all, largely what we were. We were all people that had made ourselves, or each other, up, based on the books we had read. What other way, I wanted to ask, is there to negotiate the real? What other way to be? But it was too late, I was too tired and too drunk. I tried not to panic about the thought that I still had another four lectures to go.

"So what can they tell us, the dead?"

"I have no idea, Fausto, I have no idea."

"Perhaps not, but you know which book you should talk about next, don't you?"

I have little time for Squattrinato, but sometimes he has his uses. We spent the rest of the evening piecing the book together from memory, and explaining it to Ana, and I went home feeling the day hadn't been a complete loss. I had my next lecture.

The Mirror of Naples by Marina Esposito

It was death that took me back to Naples, as I had always known it would be. Mother called early in the morning; I don't think she had any idea of the time difference.

"Your brother's dead," she said.

"I know, Mother. He died ten years ago."

"So explain to me why I've just seen him walking down the street." It was a difficult time for the city, that summer, not that there's any other kind of time for the Neapolitans. They might be the most self-pitying and sentimental people I know (and I can say that because, hell, I'm one of them after all), but the city I'd left a decade ago was choking on its own self-spun tangle of corruption and lies. It still was. It still is. I knew I'd never be able to get far enough away to escape.

Mother had become convinced that due to the semi-permanent rubbish crisis, the munnezza piled person-high on the sidewalks, all the sewers had become so blocked that they were backing up, spewing their unique cargo of shit and gold right back onto the streets from whence it had come. This included the dead. My

*brother's body, after all, had never been found, and it was highly
likely that it had been stuffed into a drainage conduit or lobbed
into the sea.*

It's a good opening, its conversational style intimate enough to cushion the shocking information it gives: a revenant sibling, a crazed mother, hints of a violent death in a violent city. The beginning of the book continues in this way for a little longer, offering up a few personal details about the narrator, describing her eventual passage back to the Parthenopean city in an attempt to sort out whatever is happening. The book, however, soon switches into a rather different register, one of its defining characteristics. Let me continue.

*In Naples, if you ever lose something in your house, there's one
thing to say, "There's a munaciello in this house." The munaciello
is a house spirit, neither benign nor malign, but one that comes
into your home at night to make quiet mischief. Few have ever
seen a munaciello, but if they have, the sight is always the same:
a childlike figure, short of stature and thin of limb, usually with
dark hair and pale skin, dressed in a white cowl or sheet and
holding a candle. A solemn guise for a playful spirit, a tiny monk
(hence the name).*

*Of course, the munacielli are and aren't, they exist and they don't
exist. Non e' vero, ma ci credo as a Neapolitan might say: it's not
true, but I believe in it. They're liminal creatures in many ways:
existing only in doorways, passages and tunnels, only at night,
only ever half-glimpsed, real because we believe and tell stories
about them, unreal because, well, they don't exist. But yet they
do: the truth about the munaciello is, as the truth often is, both
more prosaic and infinitely more fascinating than the stories.*

The city of Naples is underlaid with a network of caverns, cisterns, tunnels, galleries and closed-off chambers. There are many reasons for this: places to hide in times of invasion, conduits for water in a city bounded by the sea to one side and volcanos to the others, ancient streets built over many times but which still exist beneath their modern-day counterparts, hiding places for brigands, thieves, rebels and partisans. In his novel La porte des Enfers the French writer Laurent Gaudé claims a gateway to hell lies beneath the Piazza del Carmine. Naples—like many big cities—is also a place marked by great divisions of wealth: even today, grand palazzi (many crumbling) line the streets of some of the darkest parts of town. To get into one of these opulent homes of the rich, it was necessary to go down into one of the subterranean tunnels, crawl through it to then emerge from the well in the courtyard that was so often at the centre of the large old palazzi with heavy locked doors. Of course, this wasn't as easy as it sounds: many of the tunnels are low-ceilinged, narrow, blocked with the detritus of centuries, prone to collapse when disturbed. The only people small enough, or worth little enough, to do this were children. Thieves would send children down into the tunnels so they could pop up again, right in the heart of the house to do or take what they liked.

It's a fascinating passage, but so markedly different from the opening of the book one may wonder if it indeed belongs to the same book at all. Which, in fact, as we shall see, it may not.

The book goes on with this mix of styles and stories, a bizarre game of doublings and counterfeits, frauds and mirrors, coincidences and ruptures, often losing its own plot and then seemingly inventing another one on the spot to compensate for the loss of the first, digging its way into and then out of a labyrinth of tunnels and mirrors,

all the while running the gamut of registers from crime thriller to
tourist guide to historical tract to philosophical treatise. We come
across the crisscrossing stories of Giordano Bruno (the poet,
philosopher, spy and heretic, burned at the stake in Rome's Campo
de' Fiori where an enigmatically cowled statue of him still stands, as
if he were a fully grown munaciello) and John Dee (*Il mago scozzese*)
and his Black Mirror of polished obsidian which—he claimed—could
transport him from one time and place to any other. We are told of
the *Sala dei Specchi*, or hall of mirrors, in the grotesquely tasteless
Bourbon palace at Capodimonte, and of the whereabouts of the
"Mirror of Naples," a fantastically valuable diamond crafted in the
city, gifted by Louis XII of France to Mary Tudor, and long missing.
All this, while the narrator is trying to establish if her brother is,
indeed, still alive, or as dead as she believed. It is, certainly, in the vein
of contemporaries and countrymen Calvino and Eco, and probably
influenced them as much as it in turn was influenced by them, a
constant game of echo, response and re-echo. It feels not like one
book, but rather a dozen different ones that have been awkwardly,
and occasionally fascinatingly, genially, glued together. Which is, in
fact, what it may well be.

   To explain: first known as *Lo Specchio di Napoli* ("The Mirror of
Naples"), the book surfaces in Italy in 1978. It becomes reasonably
successful, garnering some minor word-of-mouth success, and is
soon translated into German, French and Swedish. However, the
story starts to complicate itself almost as soon as it begins. Less
than a year after that initial publication, the titular author, Marina
Esposito, gives an interview denying that this was the book she
wrote. Her book, she claims, was a much more nuanced work, similar
to the one that is slowly beginning to achieve international fame
and prestige, but far better. The book, she claims, was extensively
rewritten by her editor, who included all the (occasionally spurious)

historical background and some of the more magical elements of the story in an attempt to make it more palatable to a wider readership. Moreover, she has never received a penny of royalties from it, despite her (pseudonymous) name being on the cover.

Said editor, one Salvatore Abruzzese, is duly found, only to claim that, apart from a few line edits, he made no changes to the original manuscript. Another smaller publisher then pops up saying that the book as printed contains large parts of a book on their list bearing a similar title, *Specchi di Napoli* ("Mirrors of Naples") but which was merely a standard run-through of lesser-known aspects of the city's rich folklore. A mix-up at the printer's is blamed. Soon after, Abruzzese changes his story, claiming that the published book is the work he originally received, but that the woman called "Marina Esposito" decrying his involvement was not the owner of the pseudonym, that the original author was another woman, Marianna del Bosco. No "Marianna del Bosco" can be found in Naples. It goes on.

This already complex situation was (and still is) further complicated by the fact that various cavalier publishers in the city soon started producing pirated versions of the book: the *bancarelle* outside the central station, usually laden with cookery books, dodgy soft porn or openly photocopied university and high school texts, found themselves piled high with badly printed versions of *Lo Specchio*. While the cover was largely the same, it soon turned out that the text in many of these pirate versions was completely different from that available in more reputable bookstores. Moreover, as reports came back it seemed the version translated into German was significantly different from the one translated into French, which in turn differed from that of the Swedish. (This tangle was artfully parodied by Italo Calvino in *If on a Winter's Night a Traveller*, but even he balked at going on as to the full complexity of the situation.)

Tracing through the various newspapers and gossip columns

of the time, trying to track down the people involved in the story, has thrown scarce clarification on the subject, with many of those involved now claiming that they remember little of the incident, now over forty years back. If there ever even was an "original" of this book, the only thing certain is that it will never be found.

So there I was, knowing everything and knowing nothing, lost in a city I had once known better than my own skin, wandering among the narrow streets that shifted before me: where once there had been a crossroads there was now a dead end, where once there had been a dead end there now opened a new street, one I had never seen before. The light was failing rapidly and time was running, but I knew I'd be there forever, no matter how far I travelled. Up above me, I could hear voices passing back and forth across the street, coming from unseen people huddled on their balconies or perhaps from the buildings themselves. Listen, said the whispers, listen.

It is a frustrating ending, but there again, what ending isn't?
Thank you.

T HE NEXT THING I remember we were speeding along the
inner highway, running a ring round the old centre, six or
seven of us packed in a cab, maybe more, Jan driving, cursing
his head off, the windows open despite the cold and music ham-
mering from the stereo in time with the roar of worn tyres on
the potholed road. Everybody laughed as we hit another bump
and something spilled and Jan swerved then hit the gas pedal
again. The night was singing, all crackle and spark, as fizzing
and sweet as the stuff in the bottles passed from front to back-
seat and back again, the ragtag crew Squattrinato had picked up
yelling directions at Jan while Jan swore and sang and ignored
them.

The Lada-like screeched to a halt and sent all of us flying
out of its doors, magically, perfectly, right outside the ?, where I
could have guessed we'd been headed all along. There was surely
no other bar in the city and no need for one either. This place
was perfect, its doors ever-open, its bar ever-stocked, pints of the
black beer or shots of the clear Zapovit with which I had made
such good friends ever-ready.

All the tables had been pulled back and stacked haphazardly
around the walls to make space for a few dodgy looking chan-
cers with half-inched instruments who were belting out a tune-
shaped racket on a scratched double-bass, a wheezing accordion
and a scrapy violin, drinkers and dancers providing percussion

by banging on plates, glasses, ashtrays, tables, the floor, each other's bodies. This was rough music, dirt music, music with one leg, and it sounded perfect.

"I thought I'd have a leaving do," said Fausto. One of his new friends (and here, I have to ask: How come some people are so adept at the art of forging friendships, and others so hopeless?) stuck an arm around his waist and dragged him into the crowd.

"Off again?" I asked when he reappeared.

"You know me, I can't stay long. Work to do." I knew better than to ask him where he was going, sure I'd find out sooner or later.

We soon got into arguing, all of us, in that way that happens with fury and friendship when you have too many people who have the same passions and too much drink. This was a constant with Squattrinato, ever the belligerent drunk, who would get himself forgiven in the morning.

"Great book that, *The Mirror of Naples*. Excellent choice."

"I thought it sounded like crap."

"I've never read it."

"I'd never heard of it."

"I've never read it, but I've read *of* it."

"Probably the same thing in this case." The group ebbed and flowed around the twin foci of Ana and Squattrinato, gathering, splitting, re-forming. It was dark in the ?, and given the hour and the drink, hard to make out who anyone was. I hovered, shifted, eavesdropped, butted in, butted out. I'd forgotten being part of a crowd. I'd forgotten *how* to be part of a crowd. I'd forgotten people were just as good as books, and sometimes, I have to admit, better.

"I didn't like the ending."

"Of the book, or the lecture?"

"Either. Both."

"Nobody likes the ending."

"Nobody likes endings." The discussion swerved and lurched more rapidly than Jan's Lada-like.

"Endings of books are always messy, badly done, unsatisfying."

"They're the hardest part to get right."

"We don't like endings because we don't like death." Someone, at some point, always brings this up.

"The ontological inevitability of teleology."

"You sound like fucking Mannbrotz."

"It's that drive though, isn't it? The narrative drive is the death drive?"

"Jan's taxi, that's the death drive."

"The end of a book is the end of a book, and death is being dead. They're not the same thing. A book should have art, and grace, and then form all that random matter into some shape or semblance or at least hope of meaning."

"But life's not like that."

"No, but books are. Books are not life: a common misconception."

(I have two important things to point out here. Firstly, I would like to say that I rarely have conversations like this: much as I would like the reader to imagine my every evening is spent with such a convivial and intelligent crowd, it is not. Even were it so, I suspect I should find such a crowd very annoying very rapidly. Secondly, I do not have perfect recall of conversations, especially when drink has been taken. The conversations recounted here are a reconstruction from what was jotted in my notebook that evening, the collaborative endeavour of those on whose assistance I have been able to call, and my fuzzy memory.)

"We want to delay the end of a book because we want to

delay death." That was Squattrinato, probably. The statement has the air of one of his pronouncements.

"What about poems then?"

"Poems have no end. They only begin again." (Definitely Squattrinato, at once profound and banal.)

"I get so annoyed with plots in books. They're not like life."

"Life isn't like life."

I think I started talking about Guyavitch at this point, but fortunately the band turned it up and even our corner became part of the dance floor, a floor that now spilled outside onto the pavement, back behind the bar and into the kitchen, into the toilets, onto the tables, under the tables. The whole place jigged and swung and spun in a loping off-kilter thud.

"He used to drink in here, you know? Guyavitch." A man with a hat, older than me, white-bearded. "That's his seat, the one you always sit in."

"I don't always sit in the same place."

"You do, I've seen you." It was the man who I'd seen occasionally, the one I'd thought a philosopher, dropping in and out—mostly out—of my lectures.

"Who are you?"

"Now that's a good question, and never an easy one to answer." It was one he wouldn't answer either, dropping back into the crowd, the haze, the dark, the noise, saying only "He looked like you, you know" as he went.

Ana appeared.

"How long does this go on for?" I asked her.

"How long have you got?"

"You're not drinking," and come to think of it, I'd never seen her drinking.

"It does bad things to my head."

"Mine too. I think that's why I like it." "Bad" wasn't the word I wanted, but it was too late to think of a better one, and anyhow, I liked the sound of the sentence. "Why won't you talk about your brother?" I went on, aiming—perhaps—for "bad" after all.

"What do you mean? I *am* the brother. Ana's over there." Oto pointed across the room, but there were so many people I could make out none of them.

When I looked back, Oto had disappeared.

A woman, one of the dancing crowd, my age, tousled blond hair, leant over and started talking to me.

"*Christophe!*" she cried. "*Qu'est que tu fais ici?*" She came and kissed me on the cheeks, four times. Her French accent was lousy, but I didn't tell her this, because mine is as bad, and anyhow, it seemed impolite. I told her I had no idea who she was, but she was having none of it, claimed to have met me at an art exhibition in Belgrade a couple of years earlier.

"I'm not French, I'm afraid. And I'm not a painter."

"I know you are not French, you are German. But we spoke French then. You are a conceptual artist. *Souviens?*" I apologised again, and told her I could not remember.

"So who are you now?"

"A writer."

"So you make things up for a living?"

"Pretty much."

"How does it work for you, this life of imaginary things?"

"Not always great, to be honest." Though I don't know why I said that to her, because in that precise moment, it was great, everything was great, the room danced, the night buzzed, the world spun and hummed in harmony, and I reminded myself that this was what made it all worth it, this was why I spent all those hours locked up with nothing but books and words, for this.

The music grew louder as the band grew more numerous, then thinned and slowed as the night drew on. The throng of the crowd broke into smaller groups, retreated for corners, alcoves, the pavement outside, home.

Squattrinato, evidently drunk but with an inquisitive eye, got to me.

"Do you ever get the feeling that sometimes you're making all of this up?"

"Oh no, I'm not that imaginative. I can't have original thoughts. I can only imagine the original thoughts someone else might have had." This is all happening, this is all true, I wanted to tell him. I spend far too much time alone with books, and I am adept at differentiating their rich textures from that of lived life itself.

"Has anything happened to you that hasn't already happened in a book?"

"Nope."

"So this has all already happened before?"

"No, Fausto, no. That's the strange thing here: it's not that all this has already happened, it's that I feel *it will all happen again*."

But before he'd had a chance to ask more, or I'd had a chance to say more, the night had taken him back, and he was gone, and I haven't seen or heard from him since.

I wonder now, looking back on it, if it wasn't the effect of my ongoing convalescence that had made me hallucinate Squattrinato's brief presence in the city, that strange evening, this whole period. Or indeed, his entire existence.

Ana, or maybe it was Oto, appeared again and showed me a complex dance routine, which involved stepping on certain of the bar floor's black tiles, then the white tiles, in a stately rhythm that grew ever faster and more complex. I couldn't keep up and slunk away.

"They're playing Crow. That's the game. The one they play." Someone gestured to the chess-like boards some groups had pulled out and explained the rules to me, but I understood none of them.

I have trouble with games. I am not, as a friend once told me, a ludic person. The thing about games, I feel, is that although they may provide pleasure while they last, once finished the player is left with nothing but the vague satisfaction of having won, or the vague disappointment of having lost. I would rather read a book.

The rules grew ever more complex and the players ever more involved. The whole energy of the bar now dwelled with them. The band began to play again, a stately yet off-kilter waltz this time, building in speed and volume. The Crow players began to dance, tracing the same steps on the black-and-white floor of the bar as they would on the black-and-white squares of the game board.

"Crow is not a game, it is a dance," said the reappearing philosopher, as the dancer-players began to flap their arms and whoop. Some of them dropped out and vanished while others leapt about as if they believed they were about to begin flying.

"Crow is not a dance, it is a game," he said.

One of the player-dancers turned to look at me, and he had my face, but I wasn't sure I recognised him.

~

THE NEXT THING I recall I was outside again, walking along the street at a good clip. It was almost light, the night ended but the day not yet begun. Ana, or maybe Oto, was at my side, and we'd decided it was the perfect time to hit the Guyavitch museum.

We may have been lost for hours—I distinctly remember walking through the maze of back-courtyards, one inexorably linking to another—or we may have been there in minutes, as I say, details remain hazy, until we were walking up a winding staircase in an average block, grey walls, white steps, endless echo.

A door stood ajar on the fourth floor, no sign or even photocopied paper indicating opening hours or entrance fee, only a small enamel plaque.

"What does it say?" I asked.

"*Dedicated to the forgotten writer*," read Ana. We pushed the door, and walked in.

I RECENTLY READ THAT a certain chair, built of cheap aggregate wood from a flat-pack container, extremely common in homes across the world and possessing little aesthetic value, sold at auction for more than a quarter of a million pounds. The reason? This chair once belonged to a writer of a highly successful book for children. What does the buyer think? That placing their buttocks on the same piece of laminated chipboard as the great author will automatically permeate them with the same genius? That such genius resides in the seat itself, not in the sheer hard work of the writer, and that it can ascend through the gluteal muscles and into the typing fingertips? Of course not. And yet, I had to ask myself as we stood in the tiny room that consisted of what may well have been the only museum dedicated to the little-known writer Maxim Guyavitch, why was I so utterly entranced by the few strands of dark-brown hair carefully placed on the notepad which lay on top of an unassuming wooden desk in a very ordinary apartment in a little-known provincial city?

None of us, I would suggest, are immune to the aura of talismanic power which emanates from objects once possessed by, touched, or even *part of* those we have admired or loved. Whether we expect them to transmit their owner's spirit to us in some way or merely hope they will trigger memories laid deep and wide in the cerebral cortex, even the most sceptical among us is not immune.

Such, I suppose, is the power of museums like this, which are in truth often deadly dull. Indeed, apart from the plaque at the door and a small cashbox with *Donations Welcome* written on it sitting on a table in the middle of the room, there was little else in the supposed Guyavitch museum to distinguish it from any other apartment in the city. This is not unusual: writers' homes, rooms or places of work or study are often turned into shrines, and often turn out to be as disappointing as their graves. Despite this, I have usually been able to find some mystery or wonder in such places, though fully admit that this is probably more due to my own hard work projecting ideas onto the places rather than for any intrinsic quality they may have. Haworth Parsonage may now have its own car park, handsome gift shop and excellent scones, and be overrun by day-tripping throngs at even the quietest points in the tourist calendar, but stand a second on the stairs and listen to the tick of the clock Brontë *père* always insisted on winding, or tarry by the bedroom windows and see the granite headstones lined up outside, look at the sofa on which Emily breathed her last, and it is still possible to be genuinely spooked. In Dostoevsky's house in St Petersburg, I was sure the thick motes of dust floating in the morning sun were the same ones Fyodor himself breathed in and out, and the *dezurnaja* guarding every door and hallway the same women who watched him scribble and gamble and eat and die, as ancient then as they are now. Vok's tiny study in Hjørring still has the sea view which led me to realise how much it must have influenced the wave-like, undulating prose of his later work.

I looked again at the hairs, only four of them, of medium length, and tried to let them work their spell on me, but soon gave up and tried with the notepad instead, to scarce better effect. I had, I admit, hoped for more. At least some handwritten labels, or a dotty enthusiast to guide us through the exhibits. Although this may well have been Guyavitch's final abode, the place where he would have written "On Failing to Get to Lvov" or "Little Eli's Shoes," and perhaps even the place where he shuffled off his mortal coil, I could not be certain that we hadn't merely wandered into someone's temporarily empty house. I half-expected a pot of coffee to be on the hob in the kitchen, a sudden returner surprised to find us. I felt we were trespassing. Perhaps we were, and someone was watching us. Guyavitch's reputation seemed to draw a strange kind of trouble to it, after all. The thought gave me a curious pleasure. When I had first discovered Guyavitch, I had no idea my soon-to-be obsession would lead me into such intrigue.

Emboldened by this odd thought, I pulled open a drawer, hoping to chance across a yellowing manuscript, roughly typed with handwritten annotations. An undiscovered Guyavitch, that tenth story, perhaps.

In the drawer were two unopened bill-like envelopes, a tangle of elastic bands, some loose, tarnished coins of tiny denominations, three blunt pencils of varying lengths, a ballpoint pen which had exploded and was covered in its own ink, and a lot of grainy, gritty dust. Nothing more. I was seeking a gri-gri, an object to illuminate this mysterious work, exegesis in the thingness of a thing instead of the abstract, but I found nothing. I thought of taking the hairs but worried I would later find them indistinguishable from the other hairs dredged from the deep seams of my pocket.

Besides, Ana had found something better.

I had thought I was familiar with every edition of the stories, but although the book she held tenderly in her hand clearly bore the man's name on its spine, it was not one I recognised.

Thicker than any slim volume I knew, cream white binding. A
new Guyavitch, and Ana was holding it.

She smiled that smile she had and let the book fall open,
ever so slightly, a narrow V extending deep toward its spine.
She took it in her right hand and cradled it, thumb to one side,
long fingers to the other, then ran her left forefinger along its
lower edge, the one facing me. The pages were cut with a gentle deckle, enough to make her finger quiver as she ran it over
the lower edge, then up onto the fore edge, both coloured a rich
deep red. It gave off an odour of ferns, of waxy newness with an
undertow of bosky musk. I could smell promise and excitement.
The spine, recumbent along the palm of her hand and weighted
on her delicate wrist, held a slow page swell as the book opened
a little further, Ana gently licking her fore and middle fingers,
then sliding them down the pages to the stiff gutter. The spine
creaked, nothing more than a tiny sigh, as the book opened further. She slowly passed all four fingers across the smooth paper,
then quickly jerked her wrist to the endpapers, so the book itself
moaned slightly, then placed the moist tip of her thumb on the
first batch of signatures and flicked, slowly, delicately, through
them, one by one, each page swelling and fainting as it passed.
The spine creaked, the pages murmured and sighed with deep,
heavy pleasure. So did we.

Books, after all, are always objects to be revered.

"Look," she said. "It's been annotated."

And it had. We stood side by side and looked at the nota-
tions, cramped handwriting in black ink scrawling its way between lines, into the margins and the gutters.

"Do you think he wrote them?"

"Who would know?"

We looked more carefully, both poring over the writing to decipher its mysteries. I could understand nothing.

"Most of them seem to be about punctuation," said Ana.

"Yes—always interesting in his use of punctuation, Guyavitch."

"I love the way he punctuates."

"He certainly has a way with a semicolon."

"You like the semicolon?"

"Oh god, yes."

"Mmm, me too. It's such a rare thing, and so lovely to find someone who likes the semicolon."

"It's hard to find someone who can use it so well."

"I love how it separates, yet joins."

In the silent room, we stood and looked at the book, and talked about punctuation, and this page should end something like this:

;;;;;;; &* &* &!!!??)&%&^${~**** ;****; ***!!!! ... ...

WHEN I EVENTUALLY got back home, I decided that the books had definitely been breeding. The half-empty shelves had filled noticeably: there were copies of Herbert Quain's *April March* and Hugo Vernier's *The Winter Journey* I was certain hadn't been there before. To them, I could have added the unknown Guyavitch. It would have sat well on the shelf, its cream cloth binding would have looked handsome between the other darker, more sombre spines. But I had chosen to do something noble, and had left the book where it was. I will never know if this was the right decision, or a life-changing opportunity squandered.

Having shown me what I thought I'd wanted to find, Ana disappeared. Or rather, ceased to appear.

How strange, to find the things we think we want, then find we don't really want them at all.

Her lack of appearance left me, I realise now, far more adrift than I had initially suspected. I sometimes think I like books more than people. You can leave books, and they will never reproach you. Should books in turn leave you, they can usually be replaced.

It was dark nearly all the time now, and the temperature rarely seemed to rise above freezing. Winter had hit. The faint piano music I had heard trailing through the building became stronger, more insistent. The same half-familiar melody

repeated, changed, sometimes faster, sometimes slower, sometimes in a different key. Even though I'd had days to sober up,
nothing yet felt quite real again. I wondered once again if I'd
hallucinated the whole of the past few days. The darkness made
it probable: I love the darkness, but admit it brings its madness.
I took the occasional walk but rarely went out; the cold made it
easier to stay in. I did not see Ana, or Oto. I did not return to
the ?. I had, after all, another lecture to prepare.

~

I HAD A dream the night before it: I'd lost my papers, it was
late, no one turned up. When I woke, I was disappointed by
the sheer banality of my subconscious and had to shake off my
disappointment as I made my way to the university. The gloom
that had descended upon me had led me to choose a book of
equal gloom. I beg your patience, reader. Bear with me now.

This Dark Night Has Given Me Black Eyes
by Agnar Landvik

The poet lives on an island with his daughter. Every morning he walks to the shore and sits beneath a tree on a small cove where the waves lap at the rocks. He goes into the water, but only as far as his ankles because the water is always cold, even in summer.

The poet lives on an island with his wife, though to call it an island would not be strictly true: the poet likes to imagine it is an island, but it is not. It is the end of a long isthmus, a spindly stretch of land which is never quite submerged and which connects the place where they have their house to a road which leads to the city whose lights they can see in the distance when evening falls. There are no lights in their house: all the better, claims the poet, to see the glow of the city in the distance.

The house is large, old and dilapidated. Strips of grey wallpaper hang from the stairs, they place buckets in the large ground floor room to catch the drips which fall from the ceiling when it rains. It rains often, even in summer. The poet's wife worries about their small daughter, how she will grow in such an environment, but whenever the subject is mentioned the poet insists that this is a good environment for a child to be raised in. I am giving her memories, he says. *You are giving her pneumonia, says his wife.*

The poet lives on an island, for he likes to call it an island, with his wife and their daughter. Their daughter has not yet learned to walk. Every morning the poet takes her to the sea and leaves her sitting under the tree while he takes a few steps into the cold, cold water. The poet's wife does not come with them. The poet's wife does not like the sea. The poet's wife stays in their house, and looks at the mould growing on the carpets, and worries.

The poet lives on an island with his wife, their daughter, and his lover. The lover arrived by chance, some months ago, and at first she only visited but now she has come to stay. The poet does not tell his wife how he found his lover, and the lover does not tell the wife. At first the wife is angry, but then relishes having to spend less time with the poet, and more time with their daughter.

Every morning the poet walks to the small beach on the small cove with its solitary tree, and every morning he writes a new poem in his head or commits more of this book, his longest poem, to his memory. The poet has stopped writing things on paper, because paper cannot be trusted. Poems written on paper, thinks the poet, can be stolen or copied. As long as the poet keeps his poems and this book in his head alone, no one else will be able to steal it.

Sometimes, when the poet walks to the beach, the poet takes his daughter with him and leaves her sitting alone under the tree while he walks into the water, no more than a few inches, and stares out to sea, watching the low, lapping grey waves and composing poems in his head.

The poet has lost his job at the nearby university, and this has made his wife very angry because now they have no money. Nevertheless, his wife loves him, and she has grown to love his lover too, but most of all she loves their child.

The poet lost his job at the nearby university because his students did not understand him. In his classes he sat in silence and waited for his students to speak or recite their poems to him. Often, the entire hour would pass in complete silence. The poet believed these were good classes, and that his students had sat and contemplated, but the students complained, and the poet was fired.

The poet spends hours sitting under his tree. The poet always tells the truth. The poet always lies. Such is the way of the poet, thinks the poet.

The poet is in exile; the poet loves it here. The poet believes exile is part of the condition of being a poet. The poet tries to unlearn the language of the country he lives in: he wants to be in exile from language itself. Poems, thinks the poet, are a place to live for a man who does not have a homeland.

The situation cannot hold, of course, though the prose style does: Landvik keeps this up for nearly two hundred pages, never flagging. Nearly sixty thousand words, all divided into small, neat paragraphs, none ever extending much more than a page in length. The precise, paratactic prose becomes hypnotic, oneiric. The repetition, not only of words and phrases, but sometimes of entire paragraphs, becomes incantatory. It is a novel in fragments, of course, but one which is obsessive rather than digressive as such novels often are. This is a book which passes over the same scenes and themes again and again in a spiral rather than linear construction, with the author continually returning to the same place, the same sentence even, each time leaving the reader with a little more knowledge, adding more to the story until it becomes incredibly, almost overwhelmingly complex, belying the simplicity of its prose.

"Fragmentation" and "obsession" are the two key words to hold on to here; as we shall see, fragmentation and obsession are what the book is about.

> *The poet watches the vase shatter as it hits the floor. He has seen the vase shatter many times, hundreds of times, even though the action happened only once. The poem he will write about the vase shattering, he thinks, is a time machine, a small knot of words where the vase will shatter for ever and ever. Each fragment of the vase is a world in itself. Each fragment he will regard and contemplate for hours. Only when the vase shattered did it become complete. When the vase shattered, it was liberated.*

> *When the poet's wife cleared away the shards of the shattered vase, the poet was angry. He wanted to leave them where they were, perfectly arrayed. He shall have to recompose their disarray in a poem. When the poet's wife saw the poet throw the vase from the top of the stairs into the wooden floor, she was angry. When she asks him why he did it, the poet tells her that he wanted to set the vase free.*

The vase, its shattering and its fragments, is one of the things the narrator continually comes back to, though it later becomes a jar containing preserved peaches. The other elements: the island that is not quite an island, the bare tree, the lost job, the love tangle. All laid out, all obsessed over, all repeated, each time slowly accumulating more detail or significance as if evidence in a trial.

Which, in fact, they could have turned out to be.

If you already know this book, you will know what I am talking about. If you don't, let me explain: Agnar Landvik's *This Dark Night Has Given Me Black Eyes* is not only a book *about* a man who lives in a dilapidated house in a remote place, along with his wife and their child, and his lover, it is a book *by* a man who lived in a dilapidated house in a remote place, along with his wife and their child, and his lover.

So far, so normal: an eccentric poet with a talent for messing up the lives of others writes a solipsistic autobiographical novel displaying a colossal lack of self-awareness. I'd yawn myself if the prose wasn't so good.

But. Three years before this book was published, Agnar Landvik took an axe and used it to murder his wife before hanging himself from the solitary tree growing on a small cove at the end of the narrow strip of land where they had lived, with their child and his lover, in a large dilapidated house.

And at once the book becomes something else entirely, no longer a finely crafted literary novel with a poet's eye for prose, but a record of a violent, abusive, controlling man.

I had debated with myself whether to include this book in our lecture course at all, for in many ways it is, for once, a book that is justly, deservedly neglected.

Knowing something about the genesis of this book changes a reading of it completely. (One of the reasons I thought about not including it was to give you a chance to read it without knowing the material conditions of its production, but too late now, I'm afraid.) Can a reader still be charmed by the wonderful, assured prose while knowing that its composer was an abusive, violent murderer? Is there some inevitable prurience, rubbernecking or ambulance-chasing in the whole process? Can a book be a literary document *and* a factual, detailed progression of a lucid mind into violence and murder? Can we claim that the book is an insight into his mind, into what drove him, that it is a harrowing document of his decline into mental illness? Would mental illness be an excuse for what he did?

I admit that I do not know, and worry that I am doing everyone involved a huge disservice by even mentioning it here.

The poet's wife finds new jars to store the peaches she has preserved, and the poet shatters them again. The poet's wife is angry, but the angrier she becomes the more he loves her and the more he insists she cannot leave him.

The poet's wife is glad the poet has a lover. This way she will be safer. This way she can leave the poet, and take their daughter with her.

The poet loves his daughter, but does not want her to interfere with the fine workings of his imagination. The poet's wife worries about their daughter, and sends her to live with another family. The poet's wife tells the poet their daughter is safer then, and that her life is better.

The poet grows jealous of his lover, jealous of his wife, jealous of his daughter. The poet's wife is jealous of the poet's lover. The poet's wife loves the poet's lover.

The poet thinks of the cold shock around his feet as he walks into the water. He thinks how much he loves his wife and how much

he loves his lover. He thinks about the moon, and if it would be
possible to shatter it like a jar of peaches. He grows scared of the
moon. The moon is watching, he thinks, the moon is waiting, and
the moon will judge him.

This is where the book ends, but the story of the book does not end
here.

There are, of course, other people in the story—there are *always*
other people in the story. Of the daughter I know nothing, and I
suggest that this is for the best. Her life has its own path. Of the
lover though, there has been news.

Recently, an interview surfaced in a little-known Scandinavian
academic journal which has not, in my opinion, had the due attention
it merits. In this interview, a certain woman—who wishes to remain
anonymous—claims to have lived with Landvik and his wife during
the years in question: that is, to have been the lover. This would only
be of a certain limited interest, now that the case has been closed,
but for the fact that *she herself* claims to have written *This Dark
Night*. Far from the poet's assertions in the book itself, the woman
claims that Landvik *did* leave notes, although nothing resembling a
complete manuscript. In the interview she says that she assembled
these notes, of which there were many, and used them as a basis
upon which to write the novel *This Dark Night Has Given Me Black
Eyes*.

When asked why she had then allowed it to be published under
Landvik's name, she said that she had believed the work to be, in
essence, his, and that she had been a mere amanuensis. Moreover,
she added, she did not think that her own name, unknown and
unrecognised, would guarantee publication of or exposure for the
tale she wished to tell.

This changes everything, I believe. Should it turn out to be true (and while the veracity of the woman's claim has yet to be decided, it seems plausible to me) then—what? Do we have a novel, or a biography? Does it matter? Where does truth end and fiction begin? What moral responsibility does fiction have to the truth?

I shall leave you to decide.

Thank you.

I T HAS TAKEN its toll, I think, all this grubbing in old libraries and bookshops, the damp basements of neglect, all this talking to the aged, the defeated, the deluded and those still with hope yet to be cheated. I have spoken to many over these years, my strange encounter with John Brisling being one such example. Others had been even sadder. I had believed I was doing holy work, finding lost manuscripts, resurrecting reputations, at least attempting to witness, to remember, but I had been called a snark, had been accused of laughing at other people's failures while simultaneously failing to create anything of my own. I had tried to find meaning where perhaps there was none. I had stared a little too long into this abyss, I fear.

"Did *you* murder someone?" asked the Profesora. "Is that why you chose such a black dog story? Is it about you?" I immediately disabused her of the notion, but she wouldn't have it. "Are all these books you talk of about you?" I shouldn't have chosen Landvik's stomach-punch of a book, it was too much, especially at this point in the year, this far into the lecture course. I should have gone for something more frivolous, Eric Borstal's *The Taj Mahal Does Not Exist* perhaps, or Harlow Blade's *The Other Side of My Hand*. "Not everything is about you, Doctor." I knew that, only too well, I think, and didn't need the Profesora to point it out to me, and I told her so even as I let her pour me some more of the vile black coffee she brewed in her office.

Ana hadn't shown up to the lecture, the second one she'd missed. Not that this was the reason for my blackness of mood; Landvik's book can do that to me on its own. It was probably for the best that she hadn't come: such a gloomy tale, after all.

"And do not leave them to decide," continued the Profesora. "We want your opinions, Doctor. No 'I leave you to decide.'"

I don't have any opinions, I wanted to tell her. I have only ideas. I spot pathways, I try to make connections. I pitch signposts. I find the traces of what has been and try to trace them out of themselves. I can't tell people what to think.

"Isn't asking the right questions at least the way to start?" This was the only thing I could come out with, the only thing that sounded coherent, at least.

"Questions, questions, questions. Always too many of them," she said, without her customary exasperation and with what for once almost sounded like a hint of kindness in her tone. "What will extract a small otter from a big otter?"

"I have no idea."

"A small otter!"

I had not, I admit, even suspected that the Profesora had a human side, that there were even the tiniest reservoirs of sentiment or tenderness in her. It would turn out that I was wrong, to a certain degree anyhow. I have, I own, possibly misrepresented the Profesora. It is too easy, sometimes, to make such people figures of fun. I knew so little of her.

"You are all rat in the riverbank today. Come, we walk. Is not safe in here anyways."

~

THE JORIS JARDVAL Museum of Popular Art stood close by the university, though I had never noticed it until now. It wasn't so much a building as an amalgam of museumly gestures haphazardly thrown together by an underpaid apprentice architect long over-deadline late on a Friday evening before he could knock off and go to the pub, his plan hastily approved by a clique of municipal burghers sitting around a council subcommittee table, each carefully calculating the kickbacks they could expect from the deal, then executed by a team of underpaid builders who had accidentally reversed the plans so that narrow backstairs greeted the visitor while a grand sweeping staircase led out to the bins at the back. Their boss had pocketed the money and done a quick switch: brick for granite, aggregate for marble, chipboard for oak and cement for everything else. No sign heralded the building's purpose: perhaps the reason I had never noticed it, or perhaps—given the strange architectural disposition of this city—it had shifted itself here from somewhere else.

"Museum of Popular Art is not so popular," said the Profesora, her voice echoing around the dusty and entirely vacant hallway as we entered. "It is not a good museum. But it is important. By important I mean, hmm, *interesting*. Though no, perhaps not *interesting*, no. It is not so interesting. Educational, yes. In its way, I suppose."

We walked through the Hall of the Wooden Gods, a long gallery featuring the country's original pagan masters, crudely hewn anthropomorphic sculptures with massive eyes painted in ash and fox's blood. "Belief still persists in the countryside. Very backward," the Profesora said. I wondered why we had come here to talk. "Safer here," she whispered. "And no one else around." This was certainly true, though as we walked along the deserted gallery, I couldn't be sure that the Wooden Gods were not, indeed, alive, and carefully listening to our every word.

"These are the Missing Expressionists," she told me as we

moved into a smaller gallery. "From a difficult period in our small country's history. These artists were influenced by Expressionism, but they had never actually seen any Expressionist paintings. King Ata—at the time we still had monarchy—had forbidden the importation of any visual images, so they could only read about Expressionism, and not see. This is what they came up with." They looked like an Expressionist's nightmare seen from a Cubist's perspective, oil paints that had staged their own breakdown on canvas. I was glad to move on.

"Ah!" said the Profesora with some delight, pointing to one picture as we entered another room, this one filled with bad paintings of dogs. "This is the famous *Talking Dog of Vla.* There is a rich tradition of talking dogs in our country. None of them exist, of course."

We carried on walking, through the gallery dedicated to Artistic Mirrors ("rich tradition in our country"), the room called merely "Broken Pottery" ("No one knows who made it, where it came from, or how old it is. The official guidebook advises us not to bother spending much time in this room"), into the Gallery of Local Scenes. One picture there looked as though it had been painted in the ? just the other evening.

"Ah yes," said the Profesora. "This is called *Crow Players*, or perhaps *Dancers*—'dance' and 'play' and 'game' are the same word in our language." We carried on, through the Room of Lost Things ("It is the lost property office, but there is not space in the offices, so they make an exhibition from it. Is fascinating, I think").

We moved into the Gallery of Portraits of Unimportant People. I asked if there were any portraits of more important people.

"Who can decide who is important or not, Doctor? Is that

our job? Perhaps, yes, perhaps no." I could only concur. "There is
a place, though, the Gallery of National Portraits, but it is very
small. We are not a country who has produced famous people."
I thought about asking a question, but then thought better of it.
It turned out my question wasn't necessary. "I suppose you will
be looking for Guyavitch, but there will be no picture of him
there. He did not exist. And even if he had, is not a good idea to
have a picture of him, in these times." I thought it best to keep
silent as we moved through the Special Room for the Broken
Clock of Liberation Square ("Broken during the Times"), which
also housed a gigantic landscape. "Liberation Square, of course,"
said the Profesora. "Or perhaps Revolution Square, no one is
ever sure. Experts debate."

Before long we were facing the grand stairway that led down
to the exit, but the exit door was closed and we had to retrace
our steps back through the museum.

"I hope this has interested you, Doctor, even though the
Museum of Popular Art contains little that is popular, and not
much art. Some countries have their genius in painting, or music, or food. Ours, less so."

"And where is this country's genius? In its literature, perhaps?"

"Oh no, much less. Our country's genius is only in its capac-
ity to endlessly lie about itself."

"When will I get a chance to meet the Professor?"

"It is best you keep your head in the dark, Doctor."

"I'm not sure what you mean, Profesora."

"The Professor is dead."

"Oh."

"Yes. Very dead. I apologise, I have been meaning to tell you
for some time now. But we cannot let anyone know this. It is a
knotted story, dense like pudding. Tied up to politics, and these

are upside-down turning times. The Professor, you see, was a man with many skills and several different identities." She produced a fine silk handkerchief with an impressive Jean Dubuffet motif, and sniffled into it. "There is a question of an endowment, a grant, and funding. There is the question of history, of the stories we tell ourselves and each other about who we are. Others want different stories, or worse: no stories at all. There are those who would stop our work: the pursuit of books, even in our country, is not always well-regarded. They would use the Professor's death, especially in such bizarre circumstances, as further pressure against us."

"And the library?"

"We have had to disband the Professor's collection. They always come for the libraries first. It has been entrusted to several people in the city, those few who care, those who will ensure its survival."

The world of books, it is known, can often be dangerous. As I have noted, where margins are meagre, skins are at their thinnest. Where reputations are all, and as delicate as feathers, the darkest passions sometimes stir. Yet while I have many stories about the jealousy of poets and the megalomania of novelists—as I'm sure, reader, that you have too—in all my years pursuing this lonely furrow, I had never heard quite such a story of state-sponsored intervention, and even the hints of assassination. I pointed out as much to the Profesora.

"Because it is about *pleasure*, Doctor. Mannbrotz thinks everything is about interpretation and nothing about imagination, and yes, he is wrong, and you should have told him. We move between both, there is no contradiction. What is imagination if not memory cast into the future? How can we *not* interpret, and in interpreting, how can we not imagine?"

As she spoke, I couldn't help noticing her usual strange mode of speech clarifying. The accent weakened, the strange idioms thinned. For once, it seemed, she was being serious.

"But, if nothing else, all this is about *pleasure*," she continued. "We do need our erotics more than our hermeneutics. And yes I can point to the surveys, the scientific research, the statistics, of course literature is about developing empathy, understanding others, of course, an axe to break the frozen sea within us, this is all true, as true as wood, but really, literature is about our power to be other people. And there is pleasure in that. And knowledge, too. Knowledge as important as air and eggs and sugar in cake. But money? Not so much. None at all. And this is the only thing they are interested in. No one makes money from this. So they are not interested, more than not interested: they want to stop us. Something important, that gives pleasure, that helps—but does not make money? This is not for them. They do not understand it. And because they do not understand, they want to stop it."

We headed out of the museum onto the dark streets. Though I wasn't entirely convinced by her doctrine of pleasure, by then I would have readily enlisted in its army.

"And you should be careful, too, Doctor. Have you noticed anything strange about your apartment?"

"The books keep reproducing."

"Oh yes, this happens. But nothing more?"

I thought about telling her of my feelings of the opposite of déjà vu (a sensation which, now that I have researched it, seems to have no name or even recognition—could it be that I was alone, the unique sufferer of this strange symptom?), of Ana and Oto, the music that drifted around like smoke, the strangeness of the hotel room and its collection of overcoats. Yes, it was strange, it was all very, very strange.

"No, nothing at all," I said.

"Good. This is good. You see, it is the Professor's apartment you are living in. I thought it would be a good place for you. I hope you are safe there."

Though I am a man of significant faults and few virtues, paranoia is something from which I do not suffer. My greatest fear is that I should end up a minor character in someone else's story, and not the main one of my own. And such I feared was now happening.

Even in the times that have followed, I have never been quite sure if the Profesora was telling the truth or if something else altogether was going on. Such things happen after a life of reading books. Nothing is ever its surface, nothing is ever what it appears to be, even when it is.

~

I SPENT MUCH of the next week trying to hide from my own inexplicable gloom as much as any of the Profesora's enemy agents who may have been pursuing me. I frequented the ? only after dark, though by now it seemed to be dark most of the day. I thought about Ana, and I thought about Oto. I wondered why she hadn't come to the last lecture. I wondered about her safety, and how far she may be involved in all this, or if even there actually was a "this" to be involved in. I wondered if she, too, knew that as soon as something begins, it has already announced its ending.

I tried to focus on the next lecture, to find a book which would reflect the strangeness of these times, but I drew nothing but blanks. As I looked through my notes and the list of possibles, I realised there was a good reason most of these books had been lost or forgotten.

They were bloody awful.

That was the brutal truth of it. So many of these books were so badly written, boring, artlessly put together. Most of them belonged in a deep hole. Others had a great concept, a good idea, some fascinating passages, or some virtuosic technical skill, but in the end they were nothing but artful twaddle.

I worried that I was wasting my time, that I would be found out, that Mannbrotz would have something to say about me and expose me as a fraud. I wondered, at least, if I'd be able to pocket the cheque before getting run out of town, or worse. I thought about leaving, disappearing, but realised I had no-where else to go.

The music, that lonely piano, kept haunting the apartment. Sometimes it faltered, stopped or seemed to miss a few notes, and I could never be sure if this was a sign that someone was actually playing it or if it were merely a faulty CD or skipping record, one to which its listener returned obsessively, playing certain parts over and over again. I became convinced that it wasn't coming from outside (the echo would have rebounded differently: off the windows and not the walls) and that it was coming from whoever lived in one of the apartments above me. I walked out and onto the stairs, a moment of clarity as I heard it again. I knew exactly what this was, of course, only that I hadn't heard it in so long. It had lodged in that part of memory that goes beyond logical cognition and came back to me like a scent. I knew exactly what this music was, and, as I climbed the stairs to find the source of the music, I knew which book I had to talk about next.

I awoke, for once, in plenty of time, and took the walk to

the university slowly. A strange dream had jarred me (it was about the music: I was trying to play it myself, but could not put the notes in the correct order), and its effects stayed with me as I walked, then entered the lecture theatre, placed my notebook on the podium, drew a gentle breath, and began to read.

LECTURE NO. 9

The Repeats by David Kingston

It's too dark not to have the lights on, and too early to be sitting in the dark. Outlines of all things blur, everything becomes everything else: the book the table it lies upon, the table the rug beneath it, the rug the floor it stretches over, the floor the window it reaches, the window the balcony it opens onto, the balcony the sky it beckons to.

I don't even hear the door close, soft as it is, because everything is fading and there is only the music, a clutch of notes, so precise, so careful, so gentle. They are everything, and I am drowning in them. I wish time would stop here and leave me suspended in the tiny silence between one note and the next.

But time batters on, and will not ignore me. As the last note fades silence begins to buzz and the light has gone completely.

Repeat.

The last thing I write is the first thing you'll read. The first thing you hear will be the last thing I listened to.

Here are some things that will happen in this story, and some things which have already happened in this story: a man will listen to a recording of *The Goldberg Variations* very carefully, he will ruminate on his life, he will tell the stories of the composer Johann Sebastian Bach, the pianist Glenn Gould, a certain Miss Emilie Spiegel, and his own life. Only when the story ends will any of it have any meaning, and only then can the story sigh its end, and begin again.

> *To where it begins again, to where it ends again. The pattern on the sofa where I sit listening to this, writing this: its floral motif reaches up and down, and always ends again, and always begins again, to the point where I can fathom neither an end nor a beginning, but only its endless ending and beginning again, with no starting point from which to trace either.*

A narrator sits and narrates what he hears, as he listens to the same music, music he has listened to many times before, and that he too has played many times, repeats repeating itself, over and again, a constant repeat of itself.

> *Darkness creates little mysteries in the corner of each room. I know each room in this house, and without moving from my seat I walk around it, the bedroom, the living room where I sit now, the kitchen and its white-tiled walls, the bathroom never big enough, cold and steamy at the same time. A train leaves outside, sometimes they sound so close. I wonder if she has got on the train I hear leaving, or arriving. Is it a train leaving or arriving? The same thing: the slow decrease of the sound, or the slow rise in tone as it leaves. Sometimes they sound the same, the beginning and the end. The train at the end of the line. The sight of the sea over the train tracks.*

The stuffing's coming out of the corner of this sofa; this cushion has worn thin. I don't suppose I shall bother replacing either of them now. But who knows if I shall stay here, or if I shall move again, somewhere else, start again, again? Who knows?

I am tired of moving.

It's time I was going.

The Goldberg Variations is a piece of music by Johann Sebastian Bach. It consists of a single main theme or aria, followed by thirty variations on that theme, ranging widely in style and speed. Finally, the original aria is repeated, exactly the same, but of course, because of what we have experienced, exactly the same has become slightly different.

The Repeats is a novel by David Kingston. It consists of an opening chapter, followed by thirty variations on that chapter, ranging widely in style and register. Finally, the opening chapter is repeated, exactly the same, but of course, because of what we have experienced, exactly the same has become slightly different.

I've listened to the whole thing now, little more than half an hour on the clock, when Gould plays it, but time stops as it plays. I've been listening to this music for seconds, for ever.

If you could capture one thing, one moment forever, what would it be? Not this moment, though I know this one will always be here, somewhere there will always be someone sitting in an empty room, while another leaves. Somewhere there will always be someone sitting in an empty room, waiting for another to arrive.

There are times when narrators tell stories, and times when the narrators themselves are the story. This book is both.

> *And there it is, the first sound, the first note the same as the last one, each one in its own unavoidable, incontrovertible position, the touch on the keyboard like the notes of the words I type. They leak from the speakers like the words onto this page and fill the room gently, almost visibly, each note a drop of light, a tiny pulse of pain in the shadows. Each note takes its place and forms the room around them. The room vanishes: there is only the sound, and me, there, head bowed, not looking up, not wanting to see, not wanting to know, sad only that the sound of the music isn't quite loud enough to drown out the sound of the door closing behind her as she leaves. I think there may have been words, too, but I didn't register them. I didn't hear them. I was listening to the music.*

Some books, I have found, have the uncanny effect of telling the story of your life while it is happening.

> *Everything stops when the music plays. Even though the notes seem to move so quickly, like quicksilver, against the grey shadow of this room: the bass keeping position, holding everything firm against the dazzling treble notes. One minute fifty three seconds (on Gould's playing at least), and it is music that never stops, that begins and stops and begins again, goes on forever, repeats until the end where it begins again.*

> *The quality of the recording too, despite its digital clean-up, there is something in the air. Is that something to do with the way Gould insisted on having the studio as he recorded it? The air*

fuzzy and crepuscular. I can hear breaths in it, if I listen carefully enough, or perhaps it is only the sound of my own breathing, one now with the music, with light, with this room, with this time.

This has been one such book for me.

I cannot even be sure now the sound of the music is something that is playing, or if it has already finished and I am merely re-calling it.

All stories, all books have the ability to dissolve time and space, but none, for me, does it quite as much as this book. If we can say that this book is "about" anything, and is not the thing itself, it is about lives passing in moments, and moments taking lives to pass. This book is about the impossibility of "now," but the possibility of "here." No book has ever made me feel more the simultaneous presence and impossibility of the moment.

The music I heard coming down the stairs, through the walls, hanging in the air is still here, always here, always there. Even long after I'm gone, those notes will still come down the stairs, float like the motes of dust I can see before me now, gently mov-ing on some incomprehensible orbit through the universe of this room, this house, this moment, now.

To the end again, to the beginning again.

I really have nothing else to say about this book.
Thank you.

I'D LEFT THE reader with me on the stair as I recognised the music which you now, of course, will know yourself. I should take the story on from there, and I will, but first let me give you the Profesora's customary debrief. I had known this lecture would be a difficult one, so her response did not entirely surprise me.

"Shorter than a Hungarian dog's back leg, this week. Anyone might think you were running out of things to say. Heaven forbid." The Profesora handed me a cup of deep bitter coffee, a black disc in a white circle as if to match her Malevichian black square of a headscarf, and railed with her usual unenthusiasm, the brief interlude of humanity I had witnessed the week before now dissipated like clouds following a storm.

She wasn't wrong of course: it had been an extremely short lecture. I was well aware of that. Only the most careful observer (of whom there were none, I supposed) would have noticed that the lecture took precisely 32 minutes to deliver. I had wanted to stretch it to 39 minutes and 20 seconds—the exact length of the 1955 Gould recording, but hadn't quite managed. I did think about pointing this out to the Profesora, but doubted she would have been amused by my conceptual purity. When preparing the lecture, I had realised it was short, and my other strategy was to repeat the thing, exactly, entirely. Once finished, begin again. I would have found this amusing, but doubted—again—the

Profesora would have appreciated the gesture, and worried that the notably scarce number of people in the audience would have had their patience tested well beyond its natural span. I hate myself when I lack conceptual guts.

"Poor ending, too," she continued, now deep into her second post-lecture cigarette. "Weak. *I have nothing else to say* is not the kind of thing we are paying you to say, Doctor."

Again, she wasn't wrong on her observation, though I do not feel the ending was weak at all. It was one of my best, I thought. "No wonder they're not coming anymore. Scarcer than rabbit shit during famine. Though I suppose they have other things to trouble them. Books seem irrelevant in these times."

I trundled home. She wasn't wrong. There had been half the number of attendees I'd started with, possibly fewer. I wondered how many would turn up next week. It would be the final lecture, after all, and I thought a few would come along just on the basis of that alone. I'd need to find something good.

Not that *The Repeats* wasn't. It was probably the best book I'd had the chance to talk about. I probably cheated though: there is a very good reason *The Repeats* is an unknown book. It does not exist. That is, it doesn't exist in book form: the only existence it has is as a doc file on my hard drive. It was never published. It was never finished, not really, I don't think. It was the only thing Kingston left me with before he went.

I'd known him well, you see. We'd been close friends, shared our writerly endeavours with each other as young men. Then, as so often happens, our paths had diverged and we'd lost touch. I had hardly thought of him in years when the book turned up as an attachment to an email with no other message. I'd read it eagerly, and was disappointed when my response was returned with a mailer daemon failure notice. I hadn't known, hadn't realised, how ill he was. I don't think the book was his last message as such, but perhaps a way of storing something he'd feared would be forgotten.

It was unfinished: such a book would be impossible to finish. It would only be one to start again. You can't contain the messy disjuncture of life in such a perfect form. That's what we have art for. I wondered if it had been the trying that had done for him.

The Repeats is a book lost to itself. It was duplicitous of me to talk about it: this was not fair, and I apologise hereby not to the current reader, who I hope enjoyed the lecture, at least, but to those students who had bothered to turn up that day to listen to a lecture about a book which scarcely exists. But there again, why the hell apologise? Enough of that. It was good, wasn't it? What a great story. And they got to go home early.

~

SO, BACK AGAIN: I was on the stair, finally recognising the music. For the first time, I also realised where it was coming from. I walked further up the stairs, to the fourth floor, the fifth, and then saw a further staircase, narrow and unique, leading to a single door at its peak. Though the music was as evanescent as a perfume, I felt I could trace it to the room behind that final door.

I didn't do anything about it that evening, preoccupied as I was with having to complete my lecture. (Truth be told, I didn't write much—as you will have seen—preferring to read out large chunks of *The Repeats* instead. I didn't really know what to say at all, other than give a brief explanation. I didn't think I could improve on it. Nothing else was necessary, I felt.) But the next evening, with the sound once again drifting through the building like smoke, and feeling emboldened by a couple of black beers in the ?, I once again ascended, then climbed the narrow staircase, all the time aware of how similar this was to one of my recurring dreams, yet also how different, as there was no anxiety involved.

It was a while before anyone responded to my gentle knock, and for a time I wondered if indeed there was anyone in the place, if the sound may have been a faulty recording after all, destined to play over and over again in an empty room. Eventually, however, I heard soft footsteps, and the door opened.

"Ah, it's you," said the woman who opened the door. "I wondered when you'd come up."

Before we continue, I would at this point like to make a brief aside. Firstly, let me express my disdain for cheap narrative trickery, twists and flashbacks, sudden interventions, arrivals of new characters or information, the revelation of a tawdry MacGuffin or all of the other tiresome and unnecessary creaking mechanics of a dramatic plot. There *are* great plots, of course, but they are few and far between, and unfold like a flick-knife, whirr like clockwork. The greatest plots, as I have already pointed out, are unpredictable and inevitable.

Life, as we know, does not have a great plot. Lives rarely have a clear instance of peripeteia or moments of anagnorisis or epiphany—most scarcely have a half-decent narrative arc. Moments that may seem crucial reveal themselves in later years to have been meaningless, and those things in lives that do turn out to be vital have ticked along, half-noticed, slowly accumulating their power to build or destroy without us even ever noticing. What life is really more than a random accumulation of chance and accident? (Even this story, which I am attempting to recount as truthfully as possible, I have—I admit—shaped and elided, reconstructed and refigured as best I can in an attempt to give it some coherence, where there may well be none.)

And yet, life does offer its echoes and parallels, it casually hands out chances that can seem little more than mere coincidences, and may indeed be nothing more than that, should we choose to interpret them so.

I HAD, IF YOU remember, imagined the building in which I was living, this building which housed the dead Professor's apartment, as an elegant woman of a certain age. Even though her age was uncertain, that exact woman stood before me now.

"So you're the writer?" she asked, her voice soft, her accent difficult to define. She must have been in her eighties, perhaps older. I have never been good at guessing people's ages. People, for me, fall into three categories: kids, round-about-my-age, old. "Or the scholar or reader or critic or whatever it is that you are?" The *t* was soft, as if Irish, but the rest of her accent roamed, maybe Canadian, Australian even, or perhaps she was a local who had learned to speak excellent English after listening to a wide variety of people. "The one who's doing these lectures, yes?"

I asked her how she knew.

"People talk," she replied. "My grandson's been watching you, or my granddaughter, perhaps. I'm never quite sure. I'm not even sure if I have one or two."

"Oto and Ana?"

"I think that's their name, yes. They come and go. Always popping up where you least expect."

"Oto and Ana come and go? I've never seen them here."

"Oh no, my memories, I mean. They go and come." She invited me in. She made tea. She talked.

"They asked me to look after the books from the library,

some of them anyway. My granddaughter makes sure they find their right homes."

Now, I look back on that evening with an odd sense of wonder, which I felt less of at the time.

"And you've been talking about my book as well, I hear," she said.

"*Your* book?"

"I did write one once upon a time. My name was once Christine Fizelle, though I've had a few others since then. It was a rather strange book, I have to say."

I repeat: I will have no truck with twists, turns, reveals, payoffs, or any of the other gimcrack techniques of the dime-store screenwriting school, but sometimes events just bloody do transpire with their own knotted progress and logic. Sometimes, I think, whatever weird force controls the universe lets its grip slacken and reveals its workings. I'd come to this city partly to look for a person I was beginning to suspect was imaginary, and I'd found a real one.

"I came here to hide, why not?" she'd tell me as the evening wore on. "I didn't want that second half of the literary biography. That boring bit where we just sit around waiting for prizes and death. No, I didn't want that. So I put a pin in a map, and here I ended up. Cities are the best places to disappear. Especially a city like this, one which changes every night, one where you never quite know what'll come next."

I'd begun to suspect that stories only existed in stories, that real life had no such patterns. Perhaps they do, perhaps I am right, after all, this was not a story, this was *life itself*, infinitely more baffling and with no explanation or guiding hand.

"I would ask one thing of you, though. Please don't ask me anything about that book. I am the worst person to ask. It's there, it's done, let me now move on. I remember so little of it; it was a kind of raptus. It is the work of a different person. Never listen to writers talking about their own books."

"Then who should we listen to?"

"Other books. And make sure you listen, and listen properly." There were times when I could hear her Irish father in her voice. "Never talk about yourself. Read, listen, think." She sat down and began to play the piano. "The mistake is to think there are universal truths. There are none. There is this time, this moment, the few things we know. Or that we think we know. For who am I even to tell this story? What I was one second ago is not the person who I will be in one further second's time. The words come out, into this room or onto a piece of paper, or a screen, wherever. They're soon gone. I could no more illumine a universal human truth from talking about my book or telling my life story than predict the future from the passage of a bird in flight or the falling of the grit in the bottom of a coffee cup. It's the flight, the grit, the cup. That's all there is."

"And the music? What about the music?"

"Exactly, you see. It's there, and then it's gone. Like I am, and will be—and you too, eventually."

I<small>T'S</small> <small>HAPPENED</small> <small>TO</small> many of us, I suppose, that from time to time we have wondered if we are not ourselves but characters in a novel. I have noted this before, and worried that I had become one. And yet, if indeed I were, I could hope at least that it was a good one. A *Choose Your Own Adventure* perhaps. Then I could decide. Even if I weren't to be the main character, then at least a character in one of the great polyphonic books, a book that might have fifty-two characters and no overall narrative arc.

I needed such a book for the last lecture: a book filled with fire and joy and song, one of those great, imperfect, torrential works, a book that blazed paths into the unknown, a book of *life*. What could I choose?

Of course. There was only one choice, really: I think I'd unconsciously been saving for this. Deep breath, now, as I rise from dream-untroubled sleep, greet a bright cold morning, and scurry over, one last time, to deliver my final lecture.

LECTURE NO. 10

~

AND THERE YOU have it. No one came. I delivered my final lecture to a theatre that was utterly empty.

At least I believe I delivered it: although the experience had
the appearance of an anxiety dream, there was none of the usual
frustrated panic, no speeding heart nor dry mouth, no inability
to form words. I stood alone on the podium, gathered my notes
before me, then perorated, declaimed, ranted. I gave the best
lecture ever, a lecture filled with passion and joy, one to be re-
corded in the books of the greatest lectures ever, a lecture which
would have left not one of its auditors unmoved, a lecture in
which everyone would have left and immediately written a book
or a manifesto or a banner and taken to the streets, one which
would have moved all attendees to found their own publishing
houses to make sure no such book was ever left lost, lonely, un-
loved and unread ever again.

And no one was there to bear witness.

Not even the Profesora, or Ana, had shown up.

It was, on reflection, a perfect work of art, one whose gesture replicated its essence: talking about a great lost book to an
empty room.

On the other hand, I may have stood there in silence for an
hour. To be honest, the incident still has its dreamlike quality
despite its reassuring quiddity, and I simply cannot remember,
and no one shall ever know the truth. I may have just sat and
stared out of the window.

I shan't tell you the name of the book I lectured about; it is
best left for a future occasion. I have left the space above not
only to indicate the aching silence, the emptiness, the void, but
for a better reason: I would like the reader to think of the finest

book they know that has been forgotten or lost, and place their own account of that book in this space. There are so many, after all, and you will have your favourite to contribute. That way, nothing is wasted.

Thank you.

I T WAS TIME to go.

I wanted to bid farewell to the Profesora so walked over to her office to find her wearing a Bridget Riley headscarf and putting dead plants in a box.

"No one?" she asked.

"No one."

"Not even that man who looks like a distracted philosophy professor? He didn't even stick his head around the door?"

"Not even him. Who is he, anyway?"

"I have no idea." There was no coffee, only a sad black meniscus at the bottom of a chipped mug. We sat in silence a moment, staring into the empty cups. "You'll be wanting an explanation, I suppose."

And the strange thing was, I wasn't. While I had spent much of the previous few weeks baffled, confounded and lost, the fascination of that odd place and my odd adventures there had left me strangely incurious about explanations.

What I didn't want, I realise now, was an ending. Endings always turn out to be so disappointing after all. What happened in the locked room, who the butler's uncle was, where the family secrets lie. There was only one thing I wanted to know.

"Who is Ana?"

"Ana?"

"Your assistant."

"Oh, she has a name, does she? I never knew."

L ATER, I STOPPED in the ? to say goodbye and Ana showed up. At least, I assumed it was her.

"I suppose you'll be wanting an explanation," she said.

The fact that people offer you things only once, when you have ceased to desire them, is one of life's minor cruelties, I find.

"I would never be interested in anything so dull."

"I heard you finally met my grandmother."

I tried to do an enigmatic smile, but neither smiling nor enigma are among my fortes and I was left with something between a smirk and a grimace on my face.

"We wanted you to help keep the books alive, and the stories."

"Does Guyavitch exist?"

"Who knows? His stories do. Keep imagining him, keep on making him up, if you have to. You'll get some more books. Keep them alive somehow. There are so many that have been lost, the ones that we will never know. We can't know about them, they're gone. The only way we can keep them alive is by imagining what they might have been, what might have become of them. Spin a story out of nothing, if you have to. You know what to do. I have to keep diving back and forth through the tunnels, popping up and placing things where people will find them."

"But the book you found, in the museum? It was a Guyavitch, wasn't it?"

"Was it? How do you know? You didn't understand a word of it, did you? But that doesn't stop your dreaming from bringing it into being."

And, of course, she was right. I had to make it up to make it real.

"Where are you going to go now?" she asked. I had no lover, no partner, no children nor any hearth or home to return to, no plans other than the vague one, already forming, of writing all this down.

"I don't know."

"Can't get lost then, can you?"

"Walk me to the station?"

"Jan's coming for you."

~

ANA DISAPPEARED, AND though I have never seen her since, I do not give up hope that one day she—or her brother—will appear again.

~

I CLIMBED THE stairs to my apartment in darkness. The sound of the piano met me halfway up and warmed the whole building. I put everything I had in my suitcase, added a copy of Oleg Gandle's *Islands of the Black Sea* and Grady Tripp's *The Arsonist's Girl*, then realised some of the books I thought I'd had seemed to have got lost: I was missing the copies of *Ariel in Mayfair* and *The Faraday Conclusion*. I've lost so many books through the years, though. A few more wouldn't matter. I'd often wondered if there is a place where everything we have lost has gone, where everything, including time itself, has slid down into the crack, through a tunnel and finished up. What would we find were we there? You would be reunited with things that mattered, but would realise that for so many more, their loss was no great disaster.

I took my coat from its hanger—it seemed to be the one I had originally arrived in; I was pleased to have it back. I needed nothing else.

~

JAN WAS WAITING outside, having just dropped someone off at the hotel. As I watched the passenger drag his bag to the door, he turned and bade me *Guten Abend*. The man looked familiar, but try as I might, I could not place him.

Jan was in a mournful mood, I think, though it had always been difficult to gauge his emotional temperature; he drove slowly. About halfway to the station (I say halfway in terms of time, I would never know which route he took, or even how far it actually was to the station), he drew to a halt, got out, went to the boot and retrieved the box of books he had offered me when I had arrived.

"Take one!" he said. "Present!" I looked through them again, with little hope, remembering the previous meagre offering, but there, yes, toward the back, a spine I didn't recognise. Was it? Yes, yes, it was. A book of shadow and flame, of light and smoke. Finally, of all the places. Perhaps books never really can leave you, after all.

I looked at Jan to thank him, and finally understood who he was. Wherever you are, look out for a skinny taxi driver in an orange shirt. He is a shepherd of lost books and shattered libraries, and he has things for you.

~

AT THE STATION, the room of lost footsteps was deserted. Everyone had gone, and taken their steps with them. It was darker than when I had arrived, and much colder too. The stalls selling pastries were closing, the coffee machines long since switched off. No one stood waiting to collect any new arrivals, no lovers embraced, only separated.

I didn't even have a ticket. Four trains stood at four platforms, each with a different destination. I picked the third one, found a seat and settled in.

I apologise if I have taken up much of your time. I hope only that you have not been bored, for boredom is the worst thing. But remember those who are genuinely forgotten, and more than that, those who have never been known, those who never even got to write a book which could then be forgotten.

I have preserved the lectures here with, I hope, your contribution. They're just a few of the many. I have both interpreted and imagined: we have to remember, and if we cannot remember then we invent.

Some kind soul has left half a bottle of Zapovit in my coat pocket. I pop the cap and drink to writers re-forgotten and re-remembered, to paper pulped and books downgraded, to those lost or burned or junked in skips or the landfills this train is now passing by as it rolls out of the city where all this took place, heading for a border between countries I know little of, to a city where I know no one, watching a scattering of birds wheel across the sky, wondering where the hell I'm going, what will happen next, and about to start reading a new book. Beginnings, after all, make the best endings.

I turn to the first page and this, I think, this is going to be good.

ACKNOWLEDGEMENTS

THE BEST ACKNOWLEDGEMENT this book could make would be to other books, and while an exhaustive bibliography would be impossible, I am grateful to works ranging from Thomas Brownes's *Bibliotheca abscondita*, to Stanislaw Lem's *Perfect Vacuum*, to Henri Lefebvre's *The Missing Pieces*, to Elizabeth Tonnard's *The Invisible Book*, and to Sarah Wood's *Dictionary of Lost Languages*. The reader is advised to seek out all of them.

I also owe no small debt to some of the places where this book was recomposed in moments of tranquil recollection: the back bars of the King's Head, the Plasterer's Arms and the White Lion; a spacious and welcoming public library or two; quiet coaches on crowded trains.

I should also like to thank the laden shelves of the Book Hive; a handful of friends, some of whom have made it into this account, others not; and one person who will never be able to read this book.

Most of all, perhaps, I would like to acknowledge and thank you who read this, and all those who read, and dream, and remember.

ABOUT THE AUTHOR

C. D. ROSE is a peripatetic author and scholar, at home anywhere there are dark bars, dusty libraries and good used book shops. He has studied at several fine universities in England, and taught at some of them as well. While his chief interests are pseudobibliography and heterobiography, he is mainly a writer of fiction.

. . . a book where the words—arranged in well-chosen sequence—tell the tale of those splendidly talented writers whose careers, due to an unfairness unprecedented in the annals of unfairness, sank like a stone to the bottom of Lake Abysmal.

"Invaluable . . . Rose writes with wit, playfulness and an impressive knowledge . . . Rose himself is an author to reckon with, one whom Borges and Max Beerbohm would have admired . . . We haven't heard the last of C. D. Rose."　　　　　—Michael Dirda, THE WASHINGTON POST

*Available at all booksellers that call themselves good,
and a few that don't*